BOUNCE

Be Outstanding Understand Nothing Comes Easy

Blueprints for a healthier you

ROD SIMS

Library of Congress: 1-4576147811
ISBN: 978-0-9968437-8-2

Requests for Information should be addressed to:
www.AVegasPublisher.com
avegaspublisher@yahoo.com

First Edition 2017
Trade Paperback

Cover Design and Interior formatting by Tugboat Design

CONTENTS

SPIRITUAL WELLNESS

"Diseases of the soul are more dangerous and more numerous than those of the body."
-Cicero

These days we are growing more and more familiar with the mind-body-soul connection and the undeniable necessity to keep all three parts active, healthy, and nurtured. Our spirit, our soul or whatever 'inner us' is that makes us human is probably one of the most neglected parts of our wellbeing. We will work out to try to take care of our physical, visible bodies and keep them conditioned while allowing our spirit to go malnourished and to go from day to day without consistent, purposeful practices.

I would offer: a healthy spirit is just as important if not more so than a healthy body. The recognition of not only our soul or spirit but also that of the other peoples around us is one of our most humane of rites. Historically, the visible part of people has been a barometer used by the lazy and the shortsighted to determine who and just how much they are willing to accept someone else. Though technology has provided more ways than ever to connect, we are less connected than ever before.

In my opinion, this is a byproduct of an apathetic society, godless, selfish, and oblivious to the fact or in denial of the fact that not only do we each shed the same red blood but also we each possess a soul worth saving. Kentetsu Takamori said, "What each of us believes in is up to us, but life is impossible without believing in something." Spiritual wellness is a dimension or phase of total wellness perhaps most divisively used to separate or divide masses globally and domestically. While spiritual wellness involves developing a deep appreciation for the depth and expanse of life and natural forces that exist in the universe, religion, as a tool for many, has been used in arenas apart or against spirituality. Conversely, spirituality has being used and viewed, by many, as separate and apart from religion altogether.

Spiritual wellness is described as being able to find meaning in life events, demonstrating individual purpose, and then our ability to live a life that reflects those values and beliefs. African history might call this the Spirit of Herú or the Spirit of Ma'at. Believers and followers of the bible read of the command to all be of the same Spirit, the Spirit of Christ. While spiritual wellness is probably something that not very many of us would consider as part of our total wellness program, its impact on our life is completely unavoidable. The pure basis of spirituality is being able to discover our own meaningfulness in this life, in this world and knowing and coming to realize that we do have a purpose that we are here to fulfill.

How much do you care about the part of people you can't see? What dictates how we treat our neighbors, far too often, is based on the part of people that we see, as we think about our security and advantage. Depending on how you answered that previous question, that is an insight into how you view all other people and whether or not you value them and their soul as just as important as you and your's.

It is that spirit that is within us that can carry us through anything. A healthy spirit flourishes most while taking the bumps and the bruises that this life is sure to dish out. Good care of it can allow us to experience and make ways for both outer peace and that inner peace that is called tranquility while still serving a purpose. A strong spirit, one that is nurtured and well-fed will only aid us in surviving and thriving in this life, these treacherous times. And it is only with that Divine Grace that we can face even the most difficult things in this life. Even in the face of the most difficult things, in the most difficult times, and through the most trying of days or nights, a strong spirit will guide us through it.

I believe spiritual health and wellness to be one of the biggest indicators and forecasters of a life of love and happiness or life of hate and anxiety, one of fullness or one of emptiness. We do so many things in this life without the consideration of our innermost being and wonder why the chaos exists, sometimes in that very body. Disease and illness, from depression to suicide, spiritual wellness is about discovering then maintaining the core of us in the most profound sense of our being; who we are and where we came from leading us to where we're going and how we might even reach certain goals.

As mentioned earlier, spirituality may mean different things to different people. As an example of that, some view spirituality as being synonymous with traditional religion while others view it primarily as the quality of our interpersonal relationships or an extension of our personal love for nature. The basic foundation of spiritual wellness is the sense that life does truly have a meaning and it's meaningful to you, and you found your place in it.

We're fortunate to have credible historians to help us to understand how our ancestors cared for each other and the land around them. It doesn't mean that they were perfect or by imitating them that you're a complete, perfect or final product, by any means, but as you are looking for purpose and meaning in your existence, it should lead you to strive for some sense of tranquility within yourself first. That should allow for you to be in harmony with those that are around you while you're trying to work on balancing your inner needs and what you are providing for the rest of the world. Many of the behaviors that we see exhibited by service providers and many philanthropists, for example, can be associated with spiritual health. I know, personally, though thankless at times, it is therapeutic to help rebuild that bridge between them and a healthy energetic, purposeful life.

Ultimately, many factors will play a role in how we define spirituality, everything from our religious faiths, cultural beliefs, values systems, our ethics, morals and the principles that we hold dear in our lives and keep them close to us. We may face even more challenging times in the not so distant future. This is why it's vitally important that we monitor our inner person that we take outside. Not only does that put the onus on us to improve our spiritual health come but ideally it would become infectious and contribute to our neighbor's well-being including that of his spirit.

Onye ji onye n'ani ji onwe ya is Igbo for 'He who will hold another down in the mud must stay in the mud to keep him down.' If we can show outwardly that we are grateful and thankful that we can lead meaningful, purposeful lives, regardless of all that is going on around us before our neighbors, they may seek to lead more meaningful lives as well. How we care for our soul will definitely show itself in our (in)actions before others not just in how we treat them.

If you were to truly assess your spiritual health, what would you discover? Would you find within you hope and a positive outlook despite negativity abounding around you? Or, would you find yourself empty or alone in the world and filled with anxiety? This life has a way of checking us and refocusing us through a barrage of unplanned events and sometimes shocking circumstances that allow us to get more educated about ourselves as we see how we handle the choppy, often treacherous waters. They show us where we fall short, where we are growing, and where we are maturing, including at what rate.

Long before we begin striving for and accomplishing those goals, the question needs to be asked: what is your purpose or what is your meaning for being here on earth? I believe, and I'm sure that you would agree, that for the most part, people want to live lives that matter and have meaning and purpose to them because we know that when there is mutual respect for everyone to find meaning and their purpose, there's harmony there. The byproduct of that, ideally, is that the others that they surround themselves with also find themselves with or at least striving for harmony and don't hinder the effort of anyone. Unfortunately, the only proof necessary is for us to see our world around us that is increasingly filled with hateful close-minded people who aren't living a life of meaning and purpose and the disharmony or turmoil that exist in their lives and how much they add to the lives of those who are around them.

We aren't automatically born or later zapped with anything that dictates what our meaning or purpose is so what happens when you do want to lead a life of meaning and purpose, and you just don't know how? There is no set technique, nor set mechanics but you have to figure out what works the best for you. It involves your values your beliefs, and that can be achieved mentally, spiritually and physically. I believe this can be accomplished like other parts of the program, by having a plan.

Develop Your Purpose

Imagine waking up every day, filled with the anticipation and the excitement of knowing exactly what you want to do to lead a more focused full life. Grab a piece of paper and write down your thoughts and ideas as you consider these questions. These questions are meant to help you get clearer on what your intentions are as well as further development of your purpose. Basically, what do you want and why do you want it? To be more specific:

- In what or where do I put the most value?
- Who am I?
- What do I deeply believe in?
- What do I spend the most time thinking about? Doing?
- Nothing barred, what would I accomplish right now?
- What do I want more than anything?

Now, how do you feel having answered those questions? What kind of emotions did you have while answering those questions? More so, what kind of feelings did you have while you were writing down your responses? It can be an overwhelming feeling to have right in front of you, your intentions and purpose for this life. It's been inside of you this whole time! You've been holding back on you.

I'm kidding, but mind yourself by not letting these things be forgotten now or get too far from you. Read your answers and review daily, ideally in the morning to arm yourself for the day. These are not set in stone so if one day down the road you're reviewing at your more spiritually mature self and want to realize even greater things, by all means, go for it!

We should also stay open to spiritual guidance as we seek to align ourselves more closely with those things that are best for all who would be our neighbors. This leaves us open to being more connected and engaged with those who are around us as we all strive to live more joyful, meaningfully fulfilled lives.

Ability To Reflect

How do you handle being alone? Can you or do you spend that alone time reflecting our dreading being alone? It can be a difficult situation to be in especially psychologically or mentally. Reflection can be described as the art of thinking about our faults and virtues, but it's also about how we view our thoughts and our feelings and even our emotions. It's not always a negative but if we have the ability to steal away for a few moments and think about right here and right now it can be a beneficial way of making very positive changes in our life. What kind of questions and conversations do you allow yourself to have during these most personal of moments? Challenge yourself to grow by questioning prior beliefs, thoughts, and ideals you've held. As an assessment and an evaluation tool, this is key in helping us to understand decisions that we made in the past and may play a bigger role in decisions we make moving forward. Sometimes this requires us to do some pruning and cleaning up as we let some habits and even some people go while we adopt new thoughts and new people to help support our growth.

Our ability to positively shape our futures rest upon our ability to positively reflect upon our lives, past experiences and learning from the lives of those who are around us as we try to grow as people who make better decisions and choices. Change how you think and watch how it impacts not only your evaluation of yourself but also your pursuit of goals. Many of us share the struggle by trying to balance our home lives, and our work lives already, but it's not impossible to add some reflective time. Make time for contemplation or meditation time, whatever you want to call it, just take time out for it. Understand, though, that reflection is different than your prayer or meditation time. Perhaps one of the best things about reflection is that it can fill the space of whatever amount of time you give it. Spot little times over the course of the day, perhaps those 'dead' times that are ordinarily wasted, and commit those moments to reflect, regardless of how short the time.

The when and where you reflect is not the most significant since even short time spans can be fruitful. Some of my favorite times to reflect is on a random afternoon or evening while cruising the quiet solitude of back country roads or posted up by a lazy lakeside with nothing but the noise of nature and my mind. In that stillness, I examine my core values and my loyalty to that inner most me, especially after mistakes. This proves to be a valuable tool, a preventative tool rather than just a source of embarrassment, shame, and frustration. Whether it be in bed, in the shower, or even in the middle of traffic, take a few moments in that quiet to reflect on anything that may be troubling your mind or conscience. Difficult times and situations ultimately benefit us especially if we can reframe our perception to positively focus on the positive outcomes or the kind of person we are becoming.

If it's not yet, build in some time for daily reflection that allows us to gratefully celebrate every little positive success we can focus on.

Know and Do Right

Knowing to do right and then actually compelling your body to do so, unfortunately, are not as married as they once were. Anyone who claims that this is easy is probably lying, never leaves their home, or they have no interaction with others. We are talking about more than just basic morals or ethics. Socrates believed that none of us willingly does wrong because it hurts the wrongdoer. We can get caught up in a groove of constantly making decisions based upon how they make us feel as opposed to just doing what's right. Situational ethics is the act of picking and choosing when we will align our beliefs, morals, etc. with our actions despite knowing the outcome to be less than beneficial or desirable.

I'm not alone, I'm sure, in having heard throughout my life that when we know better, we do better. While I still believe this, I would be lying and a fraud if I said that this is some guarantee or security against making often detrimental decisions. It takes commitment, a daily, maybe even moment to moment commitment to our integrity and character. Countless times I failed here. While it may seem inherent that facing a familiar challenge, even ones that we know will not work to our benefit, it still doesn't prevent us from sometimes making life draining, soul wrenching decisions that take us further away from the kind of men and women we want to be.

Socrates also believed that the most devastating part of our choices and decisions is the fact that we are often oblivious to the potentially long-lasting deterioration of our soul or character when we choose incorrectly. Sometimes we make these decisions out of selfishness, greediness, but mainly out of a place of ignorance. We don't understand or realize the damage we are doing to ourselves when we willingly make these choices that are not only against our conscience but also of our character. It's no wonder that the ability to make the right choice based on our knowledge is a very good indicator of a person's spiritual health or a glaring sign of spiritual disease.

Practice Compassion and Forgiveness

The ability to both have compassion and have it to the capacity that you can forgive someone are lost arts in what is an increasingly hard-shelled world. The things that we experience could produce an enduring, almost irreversible hardness if we were to let them. During a presentation recently, I spoke on the differences between one who was empathetic, one who was sympathetic, and of course the one who is apathetic. While I think having sympathy for someone is easy to show it is, it's an involuntary function of being able to share in the experience of the struggle or the suffering of another. Being able to identify and relate to someone, though, is based on having shared the experience, the actual emotions. This is a key, I believe, in being able to learn more about an individual and even to learn more about yourself. By no means take this to mean that having sympathy for someone is not good enough. Nowadays, you need to have someone in your life who takes the time to text you, to call you, or even take the time to see you in person.

Treasure those people. It is decreasingly becoming more of the mode since people seemingly are so caught up in their happenings and no longer truly care past the words that come out of their mouth.

The last description that I detailed was the trait of apathy. Without empathy or sympathy, forgiveness is impossible. Ironically enough, I tied that conversation into a discussion concerning spiritual apathy among 'believers.' The media, meaning the news we watch, the newspapers, and even in some commentary on the radio, it just makes for more societal desensitization. In reality, it has been shown that realizing the full range of your emotions is, in fact, healthy as it pertains to our overall health and well-being. It has hardened us and made us gloss over the major things while continuing to grasp and trip over minor things.

Nowadays, you are truly either hot or cold, you care too much, or it is perceived that you don't care enough or at all. The person who exhibits the trait of apathy is all out of emotions and feelings. Some view this as a freedom when you get to the point to where you don't care about what others think.

While I can see the benefits or some benefits, at least, in not getting too high or too low over the opinions of others, I have to believe, and I can find proof to support me in this, that typically people who are past having feelings or emotions are dangerous people, not *free* people. They may be free in their actions and those goings-on, but we aren't free when they roam among us.

Countless shows and programs document how the lives of serial killers begin to go off course early in life. In particular, I can recall several of the real accounts of children victimized early in life and how they developed into men and women filled with rage and violence while choosing base things to find victory in this life, although small and however temporary they may be. Many struggle with the ability to forgive others as they wrong us. I know of people who held grudges for 10, 15, 20, and 30 years. Mahatma Gandhi said, "The weak can never forgive. Forgiveness is the attribute of the strong." It takes no courage to hold a grudge against someone or something. Instead, it does, in fact, take more strength to forgive. It is even better to forgive before you've been asked forgiveness than to sit back and wait grudgingly for someone to come and apologize. It says more about them than it does about you at that point.

What about the person who can't forgive themselves? Sometimes it's easier to forgive someone else than it is to forgive ourselves. I know I have been guilty upholding wrong against myself over periods of time and using a bird's eye view can see how the lack of forgiving myself caused me to worsen and perpetuate certain situations often to my detriment. Before I was capable of forgiving myself, I isolated myself from others, even those whom I knew to be at least offering to help me. My attitude and my mentality wouldn't allow me to let those who I'd made victims, in mind, to help me because I was not yet forgiven myself. It leaves you in a dark, lonely place searching for answers, questioning everything. My faith and the support of strong, caring friends and family proved invaluable, and it can't be discounted when preserving spiritual strength and the health of our soul.

Unfortunately, we have seemingly fast forwarded back to a time where spiritual differences are not only dividing us, but religious and spiritual differences are being balanced with the taking of lives. As we increasingly become more of a 'spiritual' rather than religious people, we can't escape what should be at the root of why we believe or have hope.

The reality is that people and, in some cases, whole peoples are targeted for their beliefs. In my lifetime, I've shared laughter, and I've shared tears with atheists, with devout Baptists, Methodists, Wiccans, Catholics, as well as cheered with Muslims and Christians and booed with Jews, Hindus, and Buddhists. The point is, religion and spirituality are not as different as it has been made to be. The practices and some of the practitioners, however, inside of religion(s) and spirituality have the most potential to cause the most lasting damage. I don't have to be a biblical or even religious scholar to know that, yes, there are different religions and beliefs out there but if what you're practicing leads it's believers to not only think and act like they are perfect or have all the answers but enslave or murder those who don't think the same, someone must surely be lacking in discernment or understanding. Their spiritual compass is off-kilter, to say the least, as they clearly have misplaced the value of a soul, that part of us, no man can see. How much better or different would we treat one another if we could, though?

SPIRITUAL WELLNESS

0 = Never or almost never (once a year or less)
1 = Seldom (2 to 12 times/year)
2 = Occasionally (2 - 4 times/month)
3 = Often (2 - 3 times/week)
4 = Regularly (4 - 6 times/week)
5 = Daily (every day)

1. I actively commit time to my spiritual life.
2. I take time for prayer, meditation, or reflection.
3. I listen to my intuition.
4. I have faith in a God, spirit guides, or angels.
5. I am free from anger toward God.
6. I am grateful for the blessings in my life.
7. I take walks, hike, garden, or have some contact with nature.
8. I am able to let go of attachment to specific outcomes and embrace uncertainty.
9. My experience of pain enabled me to grow spiritually.
10. I practice compassion and forgiveness of myself and others.

Spiritual Wellness Score: _____

0-25 Weak/Poor/Low
26-40 Average
41-50 Excellent/High

INTELLECTUAL WELLNESS

Benjamin Franklin said, "Without continual growth and progress, such words as improvement, achievement, and success have no meaning."

Intellectual wellness intrigues us and almost forces us to engage in a constant discovery and uncovering of you. It's a hunger for a new understanding that feeds off gaining new ideas, concerning that discovery ourselves. It doesn't have anything to do with being a 'know-it-all' but more so with us surrounding ourselves with opportunities to grow, develop, increase and improve into more matured, well-rounded people. It's about our ability to adapt to and absorb new information and reframe them as helpful things because they give us a mental stimulation or challenge. Do you truly cherish mental growth or do you avoid the things that challenge your brain? Are you open to new ideas and respectful to other perspectives? Do you ever search for new learning opportunities and get some actual excitement from brain stimulating activities? How about personal growth? Do you seek it out or are you content with your present set of skills? Are you a creative or imaginative person? Be honest, how would you know if you aren't looking for ways to be creative or use your imagination?

Answering 'no' to any of those questions may indicate areas that you could stand to improve your intellectual wellness, so please keep reading.

Again, Intellectual Wellness has nothing to do with being some 'know-it-all' but rather everything to do with personal discovery on a continual basis. This part or portion of our wellness has to do with what we are doing with our brains: feeding it or letting it die. How resourceful are you? This part of wellness gives us an opportunity to look at how we spend our time pursuing our personal interests. For instance, reading books, magazines, or newspapers is a common way to increase this area of wellness and acquire new knowledge. Are you into current political issues or want new technical ideas? As we develop our intellectual curiosity, we would be attempting to expand and grow from every mental challenge and every other opportunity where we were given a chance to exhibit some creativity and imagination.

As Napoleon Hill said, "Strength and growth come only through continuous effort and struggle." According to the University of California, research has shown that the number of connections between brain cells can continue to grow if we exercise our brain with intellectual endeavors although it's been shown that the number of actual cells in our brain starts to decline in our mid to late twenties. The more challenges we present to our brains on a consistent basis the better. If we aren't using it, we are, in fact, losing it. With the acceptance of intellectual challenges, we can encourage the formation of new neural connections in our brain. Again, the longer we can keep that up, the better.

Whether you are learning a new language or trying to develop some new skill through practicing, your brain will thank you for the challenge. Imagine how you are going to feel learning something new and challenging yourself to accomplish something that you may have never even thought of approaching before. That is truly an empowering feeling that just produces more thirst and more hunger for opportunities to discover more new things, new gifts, new layers and new dimensions of our self.

Try digging into current events or 'hot' issues. Finding a news source outside of mainstream news media was one of the most eye-opening but worthwhile activities I have ever done. To get in-depth, unbiased coverage of the biggest most controversial social topics, while frustrating because 'truth' often hurts, but liberating because I felt equipped enough to make an informed decision and whether or not action needed to be taken.

Perhaps there are causes that a close to you or opportunities for volunteerism in a scholastic or community type activity. Reading a classic for the fun of it or one that stimulates your mind will go a long way toward the nurturing of your creativity. Believe me; I know the difficulty in finding time to engage in an enjoyable read in between what we have to for either work or school. If it's something, though, with no "serious" strings attached, you can improve your intellectual mind. That may be a stretch considering the things that typically occupy our thoughts. Visiting museums or attending a lecture or some other educational show, even traveling can aid in the assimilation of things learned in school and real life experience. While these experiences may be different from one person to the next, it's all about you and your ability to remain hungry for growth. Recognize and value learning as a lifelong process and tool that extends long after your last degree, diploma or G.E.D.

Actively seek out opportunities to strain your brain, for the good. Step outside of the box and let the creative juices flow.

Self Awareness and Valuing Self

More than any other time in history if you aren't aware of who you are or what you are, between the media, conspiracies, and useless distractions, it's very easy for one to lose themselves and have difficulty when it comes to finding an appropriate value of self. Measuring and comparing yourself to people in TV, the successful family member(s), or the neighbors down the street in a self-degrading way will never serve you well nor should you allow the opinions of others to determine how you feel about yourself. We can find ourselves today busier than ever but getting less of what we need to get done accomplished. I know it's difficult, with the types of schedules that we keep, to find time to think about our strengths and weaknesses and how they are reflected in the type of people that we are or that we show the world. Seemingly, we are more selfish than ever before while being just as greedy if not greedier than ever before. Self-awareness, on Wikipedia's page, is described as "the capacity for introspection and the ability to recognize one's self as an individual separate from the environment and other individuals." As we look out amongst the crowds, you see large segments of 'followers' uninformed in willful ignorance. Between the TV and the radio and the mouths of the ignorant declaring who we are supposed to be and what we're supposed to be, we tend to lose our true selves. We pursue damaging relationships, we hang onto jobs and allow the daily occurrence of needs being met to be looked down upon as something tedious and mundane.

Why do we make certain decisions? What drives you or what are some of the finer points and details of our personalities? What is it about our habits and our values that either draw people to us or drive them away from us?

Self-awareness is essential when it comes to maximizing how we manage our person and our talents or set of skills. It can improve our consciousness and help as we realign ourselves for the type of growth and opportunities that may arise either personally or professionally. While self-awareness is not to be confused with self-consciousness, we as individuals do become more conscious of ourselves through the development of our self-awareness. We are complex, diverse beings, and for us to become more self-aware and increase our intellectual awareness, we have to develop a firm understanding of ourselves in various areas. These areas ranging from our daily habits to our personality traits and our perceived needs drive our behaviors.

A quick word on **Wants versus Needs ...**

From the time we are babies, we begin to become aware of what to do when our needs aren't being met. Somewhere along the road, though, we learned how to imitate those same actions later in life, but now we use those actions in pursuit of our wants. We allow ourselves to become often bored by and neglect our needs being met and just about forfeit that blessing for what we think we want. Don't misunderstand me; I'm not saying that all of our wants are bad yet when we give that or them more energy, attention, or care than we give to our needs we risk losing the luxury of having those needs met. You may have a different definition, but to me, a need is something I can not do without, for example, food, water, air, clothing, etcétera. From a psychological need standpoint, there are some needs that are the driving force behind our behaviors. The need to be loved, wanted, and feel affection drives certain of our behaviors. That feeling of belonging is comparable of the teenage boy who's lost his father or both parents only to be sucked into the street life because he feels accepted there. Another example is the young woman who stays in the abusive relationship with the man whose former jealousy has turned violent, yet she refuses to leave after being convinced she doesn't deserve any better.

Some are driven by the need to be in charge or to have power or control over someone or a group of people. We even use terms like "power-hungry" and use phrases like "it's going to his/her head" to describe this psychological shift that takes place when someone's given a role or position or even a title for the first time. These people tend to be more caught up in what those positions or titles afford them by way of status than the grander stage to work their magic. It consumes them and unfortunately often becomes the sword left being wielded by someone unfit to even wear the sheath. Everything that they are is wrapped up in how others view them and their possession or an accumulation of 'stuff.' If you don't believe that, watch what happens to them once their grip on those titles or possessions is threatened.

Critical Thinking Critical

One of the hardest but most beneficial things to do when dealing with chaos turmoil and confusion is to keep the mind and the brain active. It's crucial to continue thinking critically and questioning just about everything. When confusion approaches our doorstep, the questioning everything part seems natural but the 'keep the thinking realistic and yet positive part' is probably the most difficult task. I know, personally, while facing some of the life's challenges, especially recent ones, there are times that I can recall when I found it difficult to keep myself actively engaged. I can still remember different settings or the different rooms that I found myself in. It was like I was there, but I wasn't there. It was almost to the point to where I left those certain settings, be it a networking meeting, meetings with family or sometimes even leaving religious services and feeling like I watched myself but was not actively present. I was not myself. It was hard to focus mainly because my foundation had been rocked. I was questioning everything and what I thought I stood for had left me laying on my back.

Without being actively engaged in those conversations, being present and putting my something in to get something out was limited. I felt like, literally for three to six months, I was walking around just like a shell of myself, unfocused and unfeeling. My days seemed to be running together. Soon I realized that it was necessary to develop some strategy to put myself back into the game so to speak. This meant reevaluating, questioning, then redeveloping as I redefined myself, my situation and the things that were going on around me. I had to step away and see just how I had fallen off and the best way to use my time and resources to get back to the old me.

Develop Your Time Management

We are all guilty, as humans, when it comes to not making full productive use of all of our time, especially when there are things bothering us mentally or emotionally or around special times of the year. Regardless of how much we hate to have our time wasted by others, rarely are we upset with ourselves for having mismanaged and misappropriated time. We all have been guilty of basically jumping from one distraction to the next without you doing or completing anything. We can get agitated about things that we have no impact or influence on. Sometimes we get just the outcome that our poor planning calls for. The negative outcomes and consequences of insufficient or no planning often lead us to deal with things that could have very easily been avoided. For example, despite my attempts to cut down on early morning stress, I'm ashamed to admit that several mornings I put myself into time situations by procrastinating and not fueling up the night before. I knew full well the night before my tank was thirsty and even in the face of a 4:49 alarm to arrive at a 6 o'clock a.m. appointment, I pressed myself into still having to stop for gas on the way or making the call of shame to someone at a time of morning many would like to forget even exists.

Worry is useless yet how much time do we spend doing that unproductively? Other times we waste time sitting regretting times, people and situations that have already passed. The point here being that time is gone never to be redrawn. I guess it would be similar to the saying about toothpaste once is already out of the tube there's no bringing it back. Why not now shift focus to how you can fill what is typically "wasted" time? That time can now be spent reflecting on the day and evaluating not only areas that you may have fallen short but also use those times to evaluate your strengths. Ask yourself "what did I do well today? Did I do anything that will help me be better tomorrow? Was I real with myself and true to my beliefs? Am I better today than I was yesterday, last month, last year?"

Problem Solving

Problems will always persist, but their impact or effects on us will be heightened or lessened based on our ability to solve them. We may have many problems but seldom can we solve many at a time. Though they seem to come upon us in multiples, we should refrain from trying to solve them all at once. The beginning of each day allows us a few moments, first to get up and be thankful but then identify a situation that deserves our energy and attention. As we're going to work or wherever our mornings take us, think of a problem to work on when giving a few moments. Logically determine how to solve the problem by identifying its elements develop a system for solving your problem. What is the problem? Can that problem be put into the form of a question and then how will you relate that question to your goals purposes and needs?

1. With the understanding that it's not always possible, when it is possible, only tackle one problem at a time. As precisely as you can, clearly identify the problem.

2. Distinguish between problems you can have an influence on and which ones you don't. Concentrate on the ones you can fix because clearly there will be nothing you can do to influence the problems you have no control over. You should be clear of the actual type of problem you're dealing with to determine what types of things will be involved in solving.

3. Determine what information you need now to solve the problem and proactively pursue that info.

4. As you're investigating the information you've collected, be very attentive to this info because you want to draw reasonable conclusions or inferences.

5. Now that you've collected your info, what are your options as far as what you will do with it? What will you do first? Is it a short or long term fix? Where and what are the restrictions working against you? Will you, realistically, have enough money or time? Do you have the 'juice' do get it done?
6. Consider the advantages and disadvantages based on your personal situation as you assess your options.
7. Do you need to take a direct action or adopt a more patient, strategic approach? Whatever it requires, move!
8. Act!! Monitor the ramifications of those actions so you can be ready to revise or modify your strategy if and when the situation calls for it.

Sharpen Study Skills

Such a vital tool in successfully increasing our intellectual wellness is learning things surrounding how our minds process new information. This means we find creative and imaginative, more innovative ways to study in ways that work for us since we're the ones that have to store this information. One thing that can be a trip up, especially when there is some test or exam involved, is to only remember the information in such a way that is only to pass the test. This leaves you with little to no memory or recall of that info passed that examination. When we can find a creative way to study that works best for us, not only will we remember more information, but we would do better when it comes to any examination because the preparation will have been made more fun and more memorable along the way.

Not everyone will learn the same way, or at the same rate, so I will share a few tips with you. If one of these works for you, then great, if it doesn't, at least you will have some idea of what direction to go in next to find a way that does work best for you.

- **Color It** - This doesn't have to be anything special. For example, red is my favorite color, so when I mark something in red, I know that it's important, urgent or something that I should remember. Green is universal to mean money so when I go to remember things that will make me money I will mark them with the green tab. Ironically in business, though, if I use a red tab or a red mark on a business card this is someone or a company I've determined I can not do business with. It may be different for you, but color coding triggers things in our minds that will make it easier when you are studying to separate topics.

- **Take Notes** - This may seem tedious and maybe even boring yet taking notes while you're reading or while you're in class or group type setting will allow you to focus on more than just what's written on the board or spoken. This allows you to put the things spoken or being taught into your memory in a way that you can remember and recall.

- **Review Those Notes** – Ha ha! Not saying that I was always very good at this but going back and studying those study materials within twenty-four hours of class, so it stayed there at the front of my mind wasn't something I was always good at. In fact, there were times I did well to go over notes the day of class, but I do know the benefit of it, and I learned later in life yes it took me until college, but I did finally learn.

- **Find A Group** - If you were one who can play well with others perhaps you already know the benefit of studying in a small group. You can find a group, and it doesn't have to be a large group. In fact, you'll probably find you work better in a small group where you can hear yourself think and hear the words being spoken by others in the group. If there isn't one; form one yourself.

- **Set The Mood For Studying** - Perhaps you've found that you need it so quiet that you could hear a pin drop before you can focus and concentrate on studying that algebra or preparing for that Bible class.

Exposure to OPP *(Other People's Process/Perspective)*
Strive to See all Sides

It's only natural after spending the majority of our early years learning and being a sponge from watching our parents, that sooner or later, we will soon need to show some of the marks of that growth. I've seen children who were babied and coddled too much develop into selfish, stubborn, and sometimes arrogant men and women. We blur the line that separates individualism from our fellowship. Just as sure as there are those times when we should hold fast to our thoughts, feelings, and emotions, we have to concede that we are all (should be) ever learning. I believe it's possible to learn from anyone, regardless of age, sex, or background. Each person today is an accumulation of their experiences, and while we can share some experiences, we don't experience them the same way. Every time you choose to ask questions and intently listen to the response, you allow an opportunity for personal growth, development, and it strengthens our interpersonal relationships as well. Listening to good advice, humbling ourselves and accepting that we don't have all the answers decreases our chances of being stunted.

On the other hand, arrogance or conceit will block the blessing that is knowledge, understanding, and maturity. Whether it be in disagreements or even just in team building situations, when we allow superficial things like sex, race, or age to rear its head divisively, we become short-sighted and do damage to those relationships.

Believe me, especially in circumstances that we immediately perceive ourselves to have been wronged, the last thing we want to do is be mature and try to see the situation from all sides. I think about some of my classic arguments with my wife, with my brother, and with old coworkers and can recall how quickly some of those arguments escalated into shouting matches and sometimes unplanned extended periods of silence. How much could have been avoided had I not been so hard pressed to prove my point or to be right? We can all be guilty of that from time to time. After all, it's only those who think they know everything who ultimately wind up missing out.

By trying to see all sides of a situation or at least remaining open to the opinions of others, we can continue our growth in the arena of our intellectual wellness. We become more well-rounded individuals, more versatile having been exposed to the processes others take to reach decisions. It allows us to remain approachable and teachable which are invaluable traits to have in a society that's growing increasingly selfish and self-willed. Without a doubt, our ability to share in the views and the perspectives of others, will either keep us on the track of enlightenment or derail our Intellectual Wellness.

INTELLECTUAL WELLNESS

0 = Never or almost never (once a year or less)
1 = Seldom (2 to 12 times/year)
2 = Occasionally (2 - 4 times/month)
3 = Often (2 - 3 times/week)
4 = Regularly (4 - 6 times/week)
5 = Daily (every day)

1. I am able to resolve conflicts peacefully.
2. I am confident about my ability to participate in intellectual conversations.
3. I am confident in my ability to be resourceful and find solutions to my problems.
4. I am confident that I can still learn new skills.
5. I am interested in learning new things.
6. I engage in intellectually engaging activities.
7. I feel that my lifelong education is a priority.
8. I am open to new ideas?
9. I seek personal growth by learning new skills?
10. I keep up to date with changes in my profession?
11. I look for ways to use creativity?
12. I engage in daily intellectual challenges?
13. I differentiate clearly between my wants and my needs.
14. I am not threatened by views or opinions that are different than mine.

Intellectual Wellness Score: _____

0-25 Weak/Poor/Low
26-40 Average
41-50 Excellent/High

SOCIAL WELLNESS

Imagine people striving to build relationships with each other as opposed to just pointing out reasons to have no relationship. What if, in the midst of an argument or some other conflict both parties or all parties involved were committed to a peaceful resolution and 'appropriate' conflict management? Are you connected to positive minded individuals who are motivating and encouraging or do you avoid people and relationships altogether? These are just a few of the questions that come to mind as I think about social health and what this phase of wellness looks like. In a nutshell, social wellness comes down to the quality of our communication and the relationships we keep.

Becoming Engaged With The Community

To somewhat steal a line from one John F. Kennedy, "Ask not what the community can do for you but what can you do for the community." To become engaged with your community means that you are not only aware of what's going on or what's wrong with the community but you're committed to seeing it healthy, safe, and striving. Far too many nowadays are content with just taking and never putting anything back. I used to hear a quote that mentioned planting a tree although you'd never sit under it. There's nothing wrong with having a little vision and having compassion for those living around us, not just in our homes. That phrase reminded me that our communities are living and breathing, that they can be hurt and damaged and insufficient to provide for those who need and depend on it.

By becoming engaged in the community, we are not just committed to the health and well-being of the individuals living there but also to keep those communities clean and safe. Imagine not just a neighbor or two looking out for one another but whole neighborhoods. Sadly, we live in a time where we don't even know our neighbor's name. I have to believe that makes it rather difficult to bond, truly support, and protect your neighbor when we can be right next door and still be that far apart. Despite the divide, I believe we can and will do better.

Valuing Diversity And Using Respect

Valuing diversity, much like, charity should begin at home then spread abroad. Unfortunately, as a country, we appear to be barreling toward more chaos over color as character collides with community far too often. Recent murders by those who are supposed to protect, serve, and defend challenges the recorded murders of the many defenseless for media coverage. Respect for others is spotty, and seemingly, we can only come together when things go wrong. I know that we have differences and some of those differences are visible yet if we were to be surrounded by no one but people exactly like us from the same place, how boring would that be? Specifically, what if everyone, and I do mean, everyone, was exactly like you? Personally, I'm glad that there's only one me. The world dodged a major bullet because of that fact. How could we learn how to appreciate God's versatility, His range, His universal care as it shows across the many cultures? It's hair-raising and mind-boggling to try to comprehend the fact that for as many people that populate this earth how wonderfully, carefully, and uniquely we are each made unique in appearance, personality, skills, and values or beliefs. This society highlights differences in calamities and redefines it as individualism when otherwise convenient.

We have managed to make those who voice an opinion opposite the norm or majority to be classified as outrageous, eccentric, or outlandish. I have always believed there to be a difference between an individual bringing attention to an issue and an individual just bringing attention to him or herself. In situations of exclusion and inequality, it is a responsibility of the 'included' or some(one) from among them considered 'equal' to speak for those who can't speak for themselves. This is not an opportunity to cry or beg for some assistance but more about being a human and caring about other humans enough to respect them and see the God and the good in them like you would hope they see in you.

Do you recognize when someone or a group of people is not just disrespectful but completely disregarding of large segments of a population? Recognizing diversity should not include using stereotypes to justify hateful and harmful actions and words towards people who don't share your same history, culture, or hue. The whole idea of treating people the way they want to be treated sometimes gets lost on some, especially the shortsighted or the ignorant because of the inability to switch spots with some and the unwillingness to in other situations. It may not always be possible, but we have to be willing to grow past the examples we see and be the example even if no one immediately stands with us. If we did treat, talk to, and consider others the way we want others to treat, talk to, and consider us, some of the crime rates, bullying, and mental health numbers might not look as grim and menacing.

Balance Social And Personal Time

How well do you balance your time between responsibility and your recreation? Do you find yourself constantly saying 'yes' to a person after person and their 'wants' only to realize you aren't leaving any time for your personal 'needs?' Perhaps you're so totally consumed by the things in your personal world that you neglect even to contribute anything socially. Failure to strike the right balance can affect both home and work life. We are either making our familial and home relationships more accommodating and peaceful, or we're opening the door for them to be chaotic and abandoned or at least minimized.

Obviously, there are some instances where the balance can get out of whack in all of our lives between taking care of business, being there for your spouse or loved one, as well as being a source of guidance and support for the children, if you have them. It takes a diligent effort not to let any of those areas go wanting or without your care and attention. How many families have been torn apart by time and distance: one of the parents' jobs keeps them from attending one of the kid's games, recitals, etc. and the eventual deterioration of those relationships? Even in situations that don't involve kids, workaholics can make their jobs their gods, so to speak, often sacrificing their personal health and well-being. Short term, the paycheck, titles, accolades can be enough of a 'carrot' and provide enough 'attention' to lull someone into a long-term lethargy when it comes to taking care of non-financial needs like proper eating, rest, or personal fitness.

There are other instances where someone's love for the night scene, be it an athlete, a public service provider, or even an assistant in the private sector, is a little deeper than the love for the job. Performance suffers while responsibility takes a back seat to liquor or leisure.

Being an almost lifelong resident of Dallas and nearly as long a lover of the Dallas sports scene, I've seen my fair share of both success and failure from area franchises. Like any other sports fan, when your team is performing poorly or at least a player or two, you want the inside scoop on what's going on behind the scenes. Historically, Big D's night life has been quite the attraction and so much so, according to Mike Fisher, a local NBA and NFL insider for 105.3, the Fan, the 'uptown flu' has enraptured more than a few of our local sports stars.

Being seen staggering and stumbling on the big game eve, late into the night, would seldom be reported or make the news decades ago. But now, it's routine, in today's *TMZ* era, to see your favorite star showing some not so wanted face time somewhere or at some time they aren't supposed to. Blowing off some steam, they call it, as a remedy for the overworked and over-stressed has long been the cry, yet I don't know that much has substantiated the viability of those claims.

Regardless of which side of the aisle you're sitting on, the necessity of creating some semblance of balance in your life for the sake of sanity shouldn't be discounted. None of us has more than twenty-four hours on any given day yet we all know people who just seem to get so much more done in that twenty-four hours than the majority of us. At the end of the day, we have to make sure we prioritize our priorities because it's so easy to be busy and not accomplish productivity.

Be Who You Are Always

One of the more challenging feats in this life is to remain true to yourself when so many people and situations are clamoring for your attention, focus, and loyalty. Discussion of our personal beliefs, culture, and background are just a few of the things that can pull us out of our comfort zone, or that can leave us in some compromising positions. Intentionally suppressing the fulfillment of your desires or obligations is not courageous if it means constantly putting you on the back burner. This not only keeps you unsatisfied, but feelings of despair and resentment are inevitable followed by anger, which is just a longer delay for you and getting back to living your life.

Along these same lines, we can find ourselves in uncomfortable or unfamiliar environments from time to time, and it may seem to be in your best interest to not 'be yourself.' Often as a kid, my mom would be on my brother and me to behave in public. Like any other kid, I found that difficult, without the usual loving threats of what would be on the other side of me forgetting who or whose I was. I was not going to embarrass my mom *anywhere*, let alone in public. That wouldn't work out well privately, so we learned early that it was a lot less painful to be who she was raising us to be, kind, honest, respectful, etc.

As we get older, we realize that it's not just because of some threat of violence for shaming our parents in public that we should be ourselves, but also because so much of trustworthiness and dependability is built upon consistency. Do people believe you and know what to expect from you? Or are you a wild card, wildly inconsistent, and wishy-washy?

I would have to say that probably the most powerful story of someone using the consistency of being themselves and winning people has to be the story of musician and author, Daryl Davis. Davis, whose controversial, yet highly transformational story of being an African American man who not only met and befriended white supremacists in the KKK but convinced around 200 of them to stop their affiliation with the hate group. For thirty years, he maintained his love for music and humanity and used humility, candidness, and some bravery to initiate life-changing conversations. Davis' 1998 book, *Klan-destine Relationships: A Black Man's Odyssey in the Ku Klux Klan,* he writes about how cold the first meetings with these separatists went and how the hate and ignorance distanced them. The most remarkable part of the story is even in the face of imminent danger and fear mingled with the formidable foe that is racism; he remained true to himself and what he stood for. Undoubtedly, had he been exposed as fake or allowed hate to pull him out of his character, it would have been even more unbelievable that he ended up with the robes and hats of reformed racists reneging on their promise to never go against the Klan. His being himself turned the iciest of introductions into opportunities for healing, peace, and unity.

Maintain And Develop Friendships

"Friends, how many of us have them? Friends, ones you can depend on?" There are numerous quotes, Bible scriptures, or mantras we associate with friendship. Helen Keller said she, "Would rather walk with a friend in the dark than be alone in the light." True friendship should never be discounted. Some friendships we have from childhood. Others are created out shared affinities for teams, schools, careers, and even hobbies. There's a quote, perhaps even a scripture that says something to the effect that to gain a friend, one must first show himself to be friendly. Be cautioned, though; the 'overly' friendly tend to find themselves being avoided. If you don't know which friend that is, it may be you.

Understandably, people grow up and sometimes grow apart. Part of what's being a real friend, also, is not allowing them to do damage to themselves. Sometimes you have to lose someone's friendship to save them as a person. As painful as it is to not have them in your life, it's nothing like losing them while they *are* still in our lives. In our apparent need to be wanted and accepted, we can keep our mouths closed to 'save friendships' when in reality, we wind up delivering them to whatever demon is pursuing them, anger, alcohol, drugs, jealousy, hate, etc. I've tried to always be of the school of thought, that I'd rather you be upset with me over me telling you a truth than you loving me over a lie. I'd be lying if I said I've never failed at this.

Yes, we care about our friends, and we even go so far as to say we love them, but as we find out, not all friends or friendships are built the same, so they don't require the same maintenance or upkeep. For example, some friendships are so strong, you don't have even to talk or see each other often, but when you do, it's like you've never left and you feel like you just picked up where you left off. Other friendships are the opposite as one friend is clingy, dependent, must-return-text-within-two-minute friend and the other is stoic, independent and 'I'll return your message when I get to it' friend. I've had good friends, and I've had not so great over the years, and likewise, I've been good and not so good, if I'm honest.

Different friends require different things from us, and we require different things from different friends but again our need to feel needed can lead to unhealthy interdependence. I read a quote I associated with a friendship that was more like a warning that said 'Learn the difference between a connection and attachment. One gives you power; the other sucks the life out of you.' We can often make the mistake of calling people out of their names; calling folks friends who are merely acquaintances or associates. Take a step back and check the status of some of those relationships. Are you mutually supportive and encouraging or are you involved in a one-sided, dependent, and flammable arrangement? Evaluate and make necessary changes where appropriate. It can be devastating to lose who you are for someone who has no interest in even *finding* themselves. Alice Walker said, "No person is your friend who demands your silence, or denies your right to grow."

While I can't guarantee anyone that they'll make true friends, I'd tell you; it'll serve you better in life treating people as if you're on the same team than to treat everyone or even segments of the population as your opponents and enemies. Undoubtedly, this won't prevent you from being stabbed in the back, being betrayed, or getting shortchanged. It may even make it more likely to happen, who knows? You control you. After all, you still can't use what one person said or does to you and paint all people similar to them with the same brush. You and I both can see the injustice that is in that attitude and can only imagine what that would be like, to be constantly stereotyped or lumped in with 'every other man, woman, black guy, white chick, tall guy, Asian, etc. I have been the butt of some of these type prejudgements.

"How can you can you hate me when you don't even know me?"

While it may seem so basic, it's so powerful and straight-forward, but this was the question Daryl Davis asked of the Klan members upon their first introductions. With a black man asking a known white supremacist, you can imagine what the response was, but Mr. Davis was resolute and obviously watched over. What followed, I would never have believed had I not seen it for myself. He proceeded to ask candid questions of these men, who had been previously conditioned and fortified with hate and disgust. The wheels began to turn, and literally, the barriers were dismantled, and a mutual respect erected. Mr. Davis, again, a musician and the author of *Klan-destine Relationships,* was able to turn sworn enemies of his, at mini-mum 200 of them, astonishingly, into friends. The former supremacists went from wanting to take his life to protect-ing his life with their own as he was introduced to staunch, devout members of the Ku Klux Klan. Muhammad Ali said, "Friendship is the hardest thing in the world to explain. It's not something you learn in school. But if you haven't learned the meaning of friendship, you haven't learned anything." Who am I to argue with the greatest?

Development Of Assertiveness

Anger and stress can wreak havoc on us as we consis-tently wake up to relationship issues, changing job status, loss and similar life altering events that force us to evaluate

38

our self-management and coping skills. Assertive behavior, itself, is at the core of our communication skills. Both our words and our actions communicate our level of self-esteem and the amount of self-respect we have for ourselves. Do you effectively express yourself and stand up for your views while showing respect for the rights of other people and how they believe?

Without a doubt, your communication style was built on the backbone of your life experiences. If you're thirty, forty, fifty years or better, it's possible, though, that you don't even recognize it. This communication style tends not to change. However, it is always possible to communicate in a way that is more effective. Improving communication skills should always be a goal.

Mutual respect can be viewed as a foundation of assertiveness predominantly because when we are assertive, we show self-respect and demonstrate an awareness of the rights of others. The way we stand up for ourselves and the things that interest us also will let others know if we are willing to resolve conflicts or add to the confusion. What we say is important, but we shouldn't ignore our delivery. When we are direct, we give ourselves the best chance to successfully communicate our feelings and our thoughts. A surefire way to have our point or our message missed is by being either too aggressive or too passive.

If your delivery style is aggressive, mistakenly, you can seem like an arrogant, narrow-minded bully who only considers self. Self-righteous and cocky people tend to ridicule and humiliate others often thinking their methods are justified for as long as their wants are being met. Even if you're one who thinks that an overly aggressive style works because predominantly you get what you want, don't get lost in those superficial wins. Folks operating out of this mindset soon find out that some of those 'wins' have the aftertaste of a loss. Being perceived as overly aggressive can leave you alone and lacking the trust and respect that many who share this attitude seemingly crave. Some might just choose to avoid you altogether.

On the other hand, if your style tends to be more passive, you will come across as uncertain, too easy going or even shy. Certain words or phrases that you use may show that you're one who avoids conflict and disagreement but unfortunately, you're also indicating that your feelings, thoughts, and emotions aren't important. This is not humility; another trait often misperceived as weakness. While you may think you're keeping down the confusion to make way for peace, always saying 'yes' can backfire on you. If you're a passive person, ask yourself if you find yourself constantly feeling like your wants and needs are being trampled on. At home, in the workplace, even as part of the team, when you don't feel appreciated, your input, your involvement and even performance can be affected. Saying yes even when you know it's not convenient will taint those relationships and the conflict it causes you on the inside will soon become unbearable as it morphs into bigger, possibly more visible issues. The stress and resentment caused from not defending yourself will turn to anger as you go through the emotional rollercoaster of being the victim and soon, your desire to get vengeance.

With that being said, now consider someone is exhibiting passive-aggressive behavior. These are the individuals who say yes even when they want to say no. They are likely to express the regret or the guilt of that by complaining about others behind their backs as opposed to directly to them. Almost as someone bullied, they won't confront an issue or an individual head on but they'll show that anger through their attitude or some negative action. You may even have grown comfortable handling your affairs this way, but before long, these behaviors cost you respect, relationships and may ultimately keep you from success and happiness.

So, as you can see, developing your assertiveness will serve you far better than being the passive person, the overly aggressive person or even that passive-aggressive character. This allows you to maintain dignity and self-respect while gaining self-confidence and more understanding of yourself. Assertiveness helps us to create more winning situations as a result of our improved decision making and communication skills. The bottom line is assertiveness keeps us from getting dogged out and prevents us from dogging out others. It will take time and practice so don't expect it to happen overnight.

SOCIAL WELLNESS

0 = Never or almost never (once a year or less)
1 = Seldom (2 to 12 times/year)
2 = Occasionally (2 - 4 times/month)
3 = Often (2 - 3 times/week)
4 = Regularly (4 - 6 times/week)
5 = Daily (every day)

1. I go out of my way or give time to help others.
2. I feel a sense of belonging to a group or community.
3. I experience unconditional love.
4. I feel a sense of belonging in a community.
5. I feel supported by my family.
6. I feel that I am a person who other people like to be around.
7. I have a strong social network.
8. I have at least one close friend whom I trust and can confide in.
9. I feel comfortable communicating face-to-face with others.
10. I rarely feel lonely.
11. Playfulness and humor are important to me in my daily life.
12. I experience intimacy, besides sex, in my committed relationships.
13. I confide in or speak openly with one or more close friends.
14. I do or did feel close to my parents.

15. I have experienced the loss of a loved one, and I have fully grieved that loss.

Social Wellness Score: _____

0-25 Weak/Poor/Low
26-40 Average
41-50 Excellent/High

EMOTIONAL WELLNESS

Are you known as the angry person? Are you the crier? Are you quick-tempered, easily rattled? Is weak a term people would use to describe you? Emotional wellness begins with a positive attitude and extends into how much self-confidence or esteem we have while managing stress, relationships, and the occasional disappointments. So many things can threaten our emotional health because there is a wide range of situations or events we can find ourselves in on a daily, weekly, and even on an hourly basis that takes us through a wide range of emotions. Emotional wellness is our ability to maintain a strong sense of who we truly are and being real with ourselves and those around us in a way that is both constructive and beneficial not just short-term but for the long run as well.

If we can recognize when we are experiencing negative and positive emotions, we can be successful in understanding why we experience them and how to handle them. This directly impacts our ability to learn from any situation and even to be able to grow from them. We can reasonably see our role in whatever the situation is and more importantly what appropriate actions to take in response to how the situation makes us feel. If we're real with ourselves, we'll be able to freely respond without feeling like we're restricted which allows us to maintain the right attitude and form the right relationships, interpersonally and professionally. Achieving emotional wellness will change your life and allow you to experience life in a fuller light. Because we are all in the pursuit of the mastery of our emotional well-being, a source of our inner strength, having a few different "vehicles" to get there is critical.

Manage The Stressors

We're vastly becoming more and more aware of stress and its impact on our health, specifically from a physical standpoint, but have you considered what it does to us emotionally? Not all stress is bad or negative nor does our response to it have to be. Dealing with stress is something that is challenging but crucial to our overall wellbeing, so it's critical to respond in a healthy fashion. Stress is normal yet individualized so when unmanaged, stress can lead to mental and physical exhaustion and even illness. If you're not one that uses stress to your advantage and thus is unable to get back to a relaxed state of mind, that stress becomes a challenge and causes changes in our body, usually for the worst. From difficulty sleeping and poor concentration to nervousness and weight loss/gain, stress can overwhelm us and leave us feeling as though our whole lives are spinning out of control.

What may stress me in my world may not be the same thing(s) that stress you out, but there are some fairly common stressors in which we share and can relate. Gaining new responsibilities while already struggling to manage time is a common stressor as well as finance issues and the various social pressures. Struggling under a load of unrealistic expectations like trying to please everyone or even being a perfectionist eventually catches up to us. Whether as an adult, a parent or as a child, beginning a relationship or even ending a relationship, all provide instances that are within our scope of reality when it comes to recalling things that disrupted our sleeping, eating and decision making processes. Clearly, none of us are exempt, that is, while we live, from having to manage stress.

Needless to say, but we can successfully manage these stressors, regardless of how prevalent or formidable they appear. Let's look at a few strategies to prevent stress from sabotaging you and/or from taking over your life.

- **Get Physical** - Let's be real here, even if you wanted to, you can't have a healthy body apart from a healthy mind. Emotional difficulties and struggles can contribute to physical illness just as physical issues can lead to emotional distress, but this can be remedied with fueling the body properly, moving our bodies on a regular basis and getting plenty of rest. Go for a run, throw some weight around, hike, swim or whatever it takes to keep that blood pumping.

- **Laugh It Off** - Life is serious enough without us taking every day and everyone, including ourselves too seriously. Laughter boosts our immune system, relaxes our body and mind while it also helps to ease the pain. They say laughter is the best medicine, but obviously many will think we're crazy if we are just walking around laughing all of the time. Being too serious eventually has its consequences as well, be it in the form of blood pressure issues or just finding yourself alone.

- **Reel In The Expectations** - Regardless of the situation, can you keep your expectations realistic? If you're still looking for perfection, either from yourself or others, you are heading toward a major disappointment. No one is perfect, yet that shouldn't stop us from trying our best and setting realistic goals. We have to remember that anything worth having is worth working for. Before you begin, already be thinking of what problems or challenges may arise so if and when they do come, you won't be caught flat-footed.

- **Make Your Goals Concrete** - If you're living this life for someone else and find that you have lost focus on what's important to you, you have to recognize your contribution to your stress levels. You can not reduce stress by living out the choices others have made for you. Get back to living now while it is present but don't neglect to learn from your past and take some of those lessons forward with you.

- **Relax** - Is whatever that's bothering you *right* now worth your health? Take a few deep breaths and ask yourself just how important is the issue. A year from now will it still be an issue? Is it even something you can change? Relaxation is our body's fix for stress. It helps lower our blood pressure and heart rate both of which stress can take through the roof. We can significantly reduce stress by meditation, massage, breathing exercises or some combination of these techniques and of course, there are others.

Clearly, these aren't all of the coping techniques and by no means am I suggesting that you adopt these all at once, but I do recommend you do something to manage the stressors in your life before they manage you. Talk to someone if nothing else. You may be surprised at how much talking to someone may help you.

Seek And Accept Help Or Support

To add to the last thought about talking to someone, I can't state enough how important it is to build supportive relationships. To go through situations that are challenging or frustrating and not have a sounding board or the security net that is someone you trust and have unbiased confidence in is a setup for overwhelm and failure. Having been a man for these thirty-six years, I don't think I'm breaking any news that we as people, but especially men, have difficulty in this area.

We don't do well when it comes to emoting or opening up to others as we tend to be more about action than talking things out. This is not always a bad thing except in those instances that those actions just add to the chaos or confusion. These are the times that a supportive voice of reasoning helps us to keep a grasp on reality and offers another perspective. A network of support can help us feel cared for, understood, and still capable of accomplishing anything. Sometimes all it takes to lower that stress is to just share with someone what's going on with you. You'll know it's the right person if the one you go to sees through your typical rote response of, "I'm good." It's one thing to know you need help and actively seek that help but it's another thing altogether to seek help yet not accept it when it's given. This makes the person who offered the advice feel unappreciated and less likely to offer it up again. Do not waste or take these relationships for granted. I can recall a quote, but author unknown that states, "We don't realize how hard someone is riding for us until they park."

Use Gratitude As The Glue

Do you typically feel content about your life and good about who you are? It's so easy to get caught up in negativity and have it blind us to how good we have it. If a want or desire for something we don't have supersedes the gratitude, we show toward the things we do have, that's the first step toward losing them. An accumulation of difficult circumstances can make us feel unfulfilled and unhappy while taking us even further away from who and where we want to be. Just as negative people can 'infect' us, positive, grateful people can also infect us so surround yourself with positive people as much as you can.

Being thankful can impact every aspect of our lives affecting every phase of total wellness. As little as you may have, there's always someone with less. Things can be worse, and things can change in the blink of an eye or overnight. For instance, while here in the Philippines, you can observe things and people that open your eyes up to how well you have it. Many have very little, but their smiles and laughter would almost make you forget how much they are lacking. They, perhaps don't even know what they're lacking! I have to believe it's because they are first very thankful for what they <u>do</u> have. Others are just as familiar with such deep poverty so the humility they show for *anything* you give them breaks your heart because you want to give them more. Earlier today, leaving my father-in-law's memorial, a torrential rain was falling, but while I was running and taking cover, a couple of kids were laughing and playing in it, laying in it, pouring cups of water on their heads. I couldn't and still can't quite put into words how it made me feel. Their toothy smiles beamed, and their belly laughs were audible over the low rumbling of the thunder and the applause of lightning that accompanied the rain.

The things that get us down don't have to if armed with the right attitude. Their existence reinforces the need to manage our lives in a way that shows just how appreciative we should be for the people and things we have instead of complaining about what and who we don't have in our lives. Make it a priority first to be thankful, then be amazed at how much we have to be thankful for.

Mindful Awareness

With so many things going on around you, you can find yourselves just wanting to be anywhere but where you are dealing with whatever you're dealing with. By practicing mindfulness, though, you're in tune and present, actively paying attention to the very moment you are in. Maybe you're supposed to learn something. Instead of just letting your mind wander on whatever comes in, mindfulness is about living in the moment. By being mindful, not only are you not letting your mind wander but you aren't letting distraction or negativity pass through your mind unchecked either. It's difficult, at times, to not get caught up looking ahead to some conclusion when we find ourselves in the middle of negative situations. You also aren't getting caught up looking behind you. Mindfulness is not just some fly-by-night trend. It helps to not only reduce stress for sanity's sake, but it's also a tool to help get us to a level of unmatched focus.

We don't have to respond to every thought or emotion that pops into our head. Mindfulness strengthens the connections in our brain that regulate how we process what we see, what we hear, and what/how we pay attention. Growing evidence suggests that with regular practice, not only are our brains altered but our body as well. We see and feel how our bodies react to stress in the form of headaches, hives, and even stored cortisol so it's not hard to understand how much healthier a body can be without that excess inflammation and accumulation of free radicals.

Being mindful helps us to regain power that is lost each moment that we aren't in control of our thoughts. This is a string we pull to detach the stressors and hypotheticals from our consciousness to arrive at a place of awareness of our circumstance with no judgment. Learn to break the habit of rote responses and take note of those thoughts as you sit quietly and just breath. If you do find yourself getting emotional, refocus on your breathing. Your mind is no free agent. It is yours. You are not its puppet but rather its master.

Angers Away

Anger is a normal human emotion, yet it shouldn't be a predominant emotion mainly because not everyone chooses to manage that anger in the best way. Anger, in general, is not a good or bad thing, but it becomes a problem when we take that normal emotion and start expressing that anger toward folks in a way that hurts them while hurting ourselves in the process. When anger is chronic, its effects can be far-reaching, damaging our tranquility, our overall health, and our relationships. With a better understanding of what anger is and implementing a few tools to keep it cool, we can keep it from being the willing hijacker of lives a bad temper can be.

The purpose of anger management is not to suppress

those feelings but, again, to understand what's behind it and communicate it without losing control of ourselves or the situation. The better we get at this, the more likely we get our needs met, the stronger our relationships and be much better at resolving the conflict. It takes work and time, especially if anger has been your bosom buddy for a large part of your life bit it will be worth it.

So now that we know why managing our anger is important, here are some tips to keep that temper from taking over:

- **Work It Out** - Exercising helps reduce some of that stress that leads to your anger so if you feel anger creeping up on you, go for a quick run or brisk walk, punch a bag or throw some weight around. Bring that blood pressure back down.

- **Take A T/O** - Timeouts work for adults too except you'll want this one. Give yourself a quick breather at the points in the day that find stressful. Ideally, those few moments of peace will help you prep your mind to handle anything irritating or angering that may arise.

- **Lighten The Moment** - If you can laugh when you feel like flying off the handle, it just might diffuse the tension. Don't be sarcastic, though that might just add sparks.

- **Forgive Before It's Asked For** - Pride is a powerful drug but don't let it cost you relationships. Forgiveness is just as powerful, and it is a necessary antidote for overcoming resentment or being swallowed up by the bitterness of being wronged. They may never ask for it but forgive them anyway. It's for your good.

- **Practice Relaxing** - What is your "chill pill?" Mine is music or sports and at other times, drawing or writing.

Having something that you can turn to for relaxation comes in handy when you feel yourself getting heated. Do yoga, stretch, breath or something to get your mind to relax.

- **Speak To Yourself Before Speaking Out** - How many angry words would you draw back if it were possible? How easy is it to spit some venom in the heat of the moment then wish we didn't spew it? Take a moment, think, rationalize within yourself then speak.

- **Know When To Say "When And Where"** - Is your anger becoming physical, maybe even to the point of involving the law? You are becoming known as the angry guy/gal at work, or perhaps it's cost you a relationship. Know when to ask for professional help and find out when and where you can go get it. THEN GO!!

Strike A Balance

Are you able to keep some balance between your family, your job, your friends and other obligations in your life? Maintaining some balance in the face of busier schedules with less down time is key in staying in our right minds. While it's unavoidable that work life will sometimes clash with home life, it doesn't have to wipe us out or leave us more miserable.

There's still the importance of making sure that we aren't just working ourselves to death but are still taking personal time for our sanity. Sometimes we have to go so far as to schedule time away to break the monotony of punching the clock, sitting in traffic and fighting with kids or spouse once we get home. Although we are stretched thin, we should remain practical and reasonable in regards to what things are immovable and the things that are flexible. When we don't have balance, overwhelm takes over mainly because we can feel like we are just pieces being moved around without any power of our own.

Because that imbalance soon can take a physical toll on us, it's a necessity that we are not only setting realistic goals but also making the appropriate things, like our health, careers, or our families, a priority. Take care of those priorities first so you can enjoy your less pressing time. Do not neglect to schedule that time for yourself.

With so many demanding and high-pressure activities crowding our calendar, lighten it up a bit by sprinkling in some activities you might enjoy. Get outside and get you some vitamin D. Listen to some music, write, or draw but just give yourself time away from really serious or pressing matters to clear your head. You can't be scared to take a break; it might just make all the difference in the world for you both personally and professionally.

EMOTIONAL WELLNESS

0 = Never or almost never (once a year or less)
1 = Seldom (2 to 12 times/year)
2 = Occasionally (2 - 4 times/month)
3 = Often (2 - 3 times/week)
4 = Regularly (4 - 6 times/week)
5 = Daily (every day)

1. I am able to maintain a balance of work, family, friends, and other obligations.
2. I have ways to reduce stress in my life.
3. I am able to make decisions with a minimum of stress and worry.
4. I am able to set priorities.
5. I am able to appropriately manage my feelings.
6. I use relaxation techniques to manage stress.
7. I am able to appropriately express my feelings.
8. I am willing to seek help from others when I am having a difficult time.
9. I feel that I am able to cope with my daily stress.
10. I have a positive image of my body.

Emotional Wellness Score: _____

0-25 Weak/Poor/Low
26-40 Average
41-50 Excellent/High

MENTAL WELLNESS

"My mind's playing tricks on me," aren't just lyrics from a 90's rap song. Unfortunately, these words describe, all too well, the plight facing one in every five people. Estimates indicate, unfortunately, that nearly 66% or a third of all people with a diagnosable mental illness don't even seek help, especially in diverse communities. According to the World Health Organization, you can define mental health as a 'state of wellbeing where an individual realizes their abilities, copes with this life's stressors, works productively, and can contribute to their community.' That sounds good and not very challenging, yet it's eye-opening (and not too surprising) that only around 17% of adults in the U.S. are considered to be operating with a full deck or to be in a state of optimal mental health. Between "America's Dumbest Criminals," the Real Housewives franchise, and the numerous 'don't try these at home' or "Caught on Tape" series, you may think even that number seems high. Evidence tracing improved long-term health outcomes back to positive mental health is becoming more and more frequent as the number of mental illnesses or disorders continues to increase as well. It's easy to see how this is a problem since we usually don't seek to address mental issues until they've announced their presence, and then the journey to save it or get it back begins.

Mental disease or illness can be described as a health condition highlighted by a change (usually negative) in thought processes, moods, or even a change in behavior as a response to distress or impairment in 'normal' function. Despite the fact that more emphasis is placed on mental illness screening, diagnosis, and treatment, the forecast doesn't look too promising as it's estimated that depression will be the second leading cause of death by the year 2020 (WHO,1996). It's no wonder that evidence shows the strong relationship between mental disorders (mainly depressive disorders) and the occurrence of chronic diseases like diabetes, cancer, and obesity. Most resources go toward treatment as opposed to prevention. It's clear to see from a physical standpoint, the benefit of preserving or maintaining physical health before we lose it but disturbingly, we aren't as willing to see that mental health is worth preserving too, perhaps even more so. Much like with your physical, be proactive in protecting your mind from mental illness, well as much as you can. Much like certain things can add to our risk of developing physical or medical issues, we have to acknowledge our role in the development of mental issues as well. Just as there are social behaviors like drinking, stress mismanagement, and insufficient sleep, sometimes there are other internal and external factors that also contribute to or take away from our mental health. Finances, relationships, and even our jobs can prove to be overwhelming sources of chronic stress, and its effects on our bodies. Everything from severe headaches and bowel issues to heart attack and stroke causing anger and anxiety can be precursors to a bout with the mental disease. According to the WHO, risks for committing violent acts against others at this point or suicide, significantly rise.

Depression And Adolescents

Depression itself, the most common mental illness, affects more than 26% of the U.S. adult population while about 20% of adolescents have a diagnosable mental disorder. Do not overlook the fact that most mental disorders show themselves first in or before adolescence with between 20% and 30% of adolescents experiencing one major depressive episode before even reaching adulthood. It's undeniable that our brains establish neural pathways during our teenage and adolescent years as we undergo significant development changes and some behavioral habits that last long into our adult years. These symptoms obviously, don't just affect how much we enjoy life but also the quality of our life. Should not be discounted how critical this time is in our lives as it pertains to not only our social and emotional wellbeing but also for our mental development. I know, personally, I can remember being twelve or thirteen with the raging hormones and recognizing how much prettier the girls were and how much better they smelled. I can't help but recall numerous stories of the jilted acne-riddled young men, heartbroken and driven and bent on revenge. The disturbing stories of bullying and shaming that inevitably lead to violence, injury, and depression sadly are becoming the norm. During our preteen and adolescent years, we thrive on fitting in, being accepted, developing plans for a future. Many struggle with the things life is teaching us and sometimes socially misconstruing situations and emotionally misinterpreting the actions of others. All of this coupled with sometimes rocky and unstable home lives can make for a combustible combo further highlighting the significance of meeting not just our social and emotional needs but also staying on top of our mental health. A quarter of individuals with mood disorders like depression has their first episode in adolescence while 50-75% experience anxiety and impulse control issues develop during the same time. Existing mental issues become increasingly more and more complex as grades, nutrition, and personal fitness can take a backseat to sexual intrigue and substance/alcohol abuse. Depressed people tend not only to try to drink or smoke away their problems, but they also are less physically active and eat less healthily. Untreated and undiagnosed mental problems very often result in more negative outcomes. Mental issues often lead to subpar school performance, which can add to drop out rate which can further strain families. Once families are involved, then the courts and juvenile justice systems become involved. It should also be pointed out that an estimated 67%-70% of youth in the justice system have a diagnosable mental health disorder (Blueprint for Change: A Comprehensive Model for the Iden- tification and Treatment of Youth with Mental Health Needs in Contact with the Juvenile Justice System).

Another startling reality is that suicide affects young folks everywhere, regardless of race, gender and socio-economic group yet some groups tend to have higher rates than others. It should also be noted that 60%-90% of people committing suicide have battled the demoralizing disease of depression. According to the National Center for Injury Prevention and Control (Centers for Disease Control and Prevention, Sept. 2007), suicide is the third leading cause of death in adolescents and young adults with between half a million and a million people aged 15-24 unsuccessfully *attempting* suicide every year.

African Americans And Mental Health

Stigma, silent struggle, mental illness, and African Americans make for a formula for slow death. Stigma is defined as a mark of shame, disgrace, or disapproval resulting in discrimination. Despite the fact that we are all at risk for mental illness or some mental disorder, communities of color have long struggled to admit the battle for mental balance. About 42 million people or just over 13% of the U.S population is African-American according to 2013 US Census Bureau numbers. The challenge facing the African-American community is not only unique from an access perspective but the treatment received is also unique. Historically people of color have faced adversity from slavery to varied exclusions rooted in racism even in the afterglow or shadow of the country's first black president. These exclusions extend into not just the health arena but also appearing in the educational, social, and economic realms. Unfortunately, as a result, socioeconomic disparities are born. African Americans disproportionately experience these oddities with socioeconomic status being an indicator of mental health or mental sickness. People struggling to make ends meet as a result of being poor, homeless, or battling abuse issues are at an increased risk for poor mental health. Black adults living below the poverty line are two to three times more likely to report serious psychological distress than those living above the poverty line according to the Office of Minority Health. To borrow an old line from *Catcher in the Rye*, "The more things change, the more they stay the same" as racism and prejudice continues to take its toll as many blacks still contend with blatant bias and discrimination while trying to pursue "the American Dream." The school-to-prison pipeline continues to ravage and bankrupt whole communities while locally, mistrust of authority continues to have a grip on its youngest residents. The older community with remembrances of historical hatred against them and the youth, alarmed at the unnecessary shooting deaths of their peers making news nationally. Needless to say, this misplaced or displaced trust can extend from generation to generation to generation with none of whom believing those authorities to truly have their best interest in mind. Imagine that impact on mental health, and you'll begin to see why it's past time to separate from the stigma of mental illness and be more proactive in recognizing signs within ourselves and in our communities.

The Health and Retirement Study, a sample which represents individuals over fifty living in the U.S. conducted a study that was released in July of 2011 that stated that while 30% of the general population reported at least one type of major lifetime discrimination, almost 45% black older adults reported such discrimination. While Latinos were a lot less likely to report everyday discrimination at 64.2%, Blacks reported the highest frequency of everyday discrimination at 82.6%. When compared to major lifetime discrimination, everyday discrimination seems to have more of a link or relationship to mental health indicators. The best way I can explain this is that it's more likely to rebound and recover from one major event than to constantly deal with something on a day to day basis.

The stigma may suggest black people don't have mental illness or go to 'shrinks,' but the stats give an eye-opening insight into the harsh reality of this imposes influence on the black community and barriers that hinder the access to services and treatment.

According to the U.S. Health and Human Services Office of Minority Health, Black adults are 20% more likely to report serious psychological distress than white adults while experiencing more feelings of hopelessness, sadness, and worthlessness. Whether you're one who's ascended the professional and socio-economic ladder or one compelled to cave under the strain of society's expectations of what a strong black man or woman is to be, the stigma still stands. With no one to talk to who would seemingly understand, this forces many in their isolation not just to feel worthless and hopeless but also have a lack of trust and unwillingness to share anything with anyone. The stigma associated with mental illness manifests itself as a barrier for not only those seeking treatment but also shapes our attitude toward gaining knowledge and a fuller understanding of this disease. Only 31% of African-Americans even believed that depression was a 'health' problem. Not only did 63% of African Americans believe that depression was a personal weakness with 56% believed that this illness was a normal part of aging. Almost 20% of those surveyed by Mental Health America in 1996 cited fear and a lack of knowledge concerning treatment and the disease as a barrier between those needing treatment and receiving it. Denial that there's even a problem made up the highest percentage at 40% while shame or embarrassment along with simply refusing help made up another 38% and 31% of responses given, respectively.

So, again, despite arguments to the contrary, mental illness continues to be quite the formidable opponent. It should be included in any conversation that arises where acceptance of diversity is being discussed. It shouldn't be treated any different than how we treat those of different religious beliefs, cultural backgrounds, or sexual orientation. People dealing with mental illness shouldn't be treated like they have leprosy nor should those who think they may be dealing with mental disease be dissuaded from getting the help they need. The National Alliance on Mental Illness has a phrase "Culture Counts," which reiterates that one's racial or ethnic background influences not just how much stigma they attach to mental illness but whether help is received in the first place, the type of help received, how much support and/or other coping styles they have.

Mental Maintenance

"No Health Without Mental Health" was the impassioned, expressed vision of the World Health Organization and their first Director-General, Dr. Brock Chisholm. Chisholm was a psychiatrist who strongly believed and argued that there could be no true physical health aside from mental health. Over six decades later, we seemingly have reverted to a time of ignorance that refuses to prioritize mental health as much as we do and have historically prioritized our physical health. Formerly, there was a commitment to elevate the importance of preserving our mental health with just as much vigor and consistency as we pursue our physical health but that foundation has sunk, cracked and is sorely in need of rejuvenation. We can all be guilty from time to time of allowing the gap between mental and physical health to exist and widen in some areas. We blame the government and other people for not considering mental health to be just as damaging to our total wellness as poor nutrition or lack of activity is but the health care system seemingly doesn't either. We work for people and companies that encourage our participation in their wellness programs that are focused on vacation time, flu shots and accumulate points for checking blood pressure or walking 10,000 steps yet they fail to motivate us toward mental maintenance. It is vitally important that protecting our mental health becomes as much a concern as diet and exercise are when it comes to preventing illness and disease.

If you were visibly, physically fit but decided to eat and drink with no forethought of what those choices would do to your body, eventually, your body will reflect that. Why is it hard to see or understand that with an ongoing script of ups and downs, twists, and turns, without reflection or emoting, our mind will soon reflect that? Life's stressors have less of a chance to wipe us out or separate us from our sanity when we have some semblance of a plan in place to prevent mental illness. You will not luck into a solution for staving off mental instability especially when there are existing risk factors that go unchecked. Our actions and habits sometimes contribute to some of the chaos and confusion we contend with in this life, but similarly, we can adopt certain attitudes and activities that allow us to protect our mental health. It doesn't just happen nor is it just fate. There is no magic pill, patch, or potion for prevention but that shouldn't keep you from being proactive and positive. Here are few strategies for saving your mental stability:

- **Remember Your Value (Accept You)** - Don't spend all of your time trying to be someone else. Get back to having standards, self-worth and confidence in yourself again. No one was made any better than you nor was anyone made any worse. Treat yourself to a healthy dose of self-respect and kindness, and it'll reflect in the actions you take and situations or people you find yourself no longer dealing with. There's nothing wrong with wanting better for yourself or for distancing yourself from things or people that take you away from being at your best. Avoid being overly critically or unforgiving of yourself. What are the things you do like about yourself or think about what is going well in your life? Stop comparing yourself to others around you and how much better someone else seems to have it. Understand no one is perfect or maybe not even happy all of the time. Be original and be real with yourself. We are all works in progress.

- **Gather 'Round The Good (Quality Connections)** - Just as is mentioned in the social wellness discussion, the benefits of having good, high-quality relationships are almost immeasurable. We have a natural inclination to want to be connected or to be accepted, but it shouldn't be at the expense of losing who we are. Having the support and encouragement of even one person can be enough wind in your sail to remind you of who you are when you forget, what you mean to them when you lose sight of your worth. They are in our corner because they want the best *for* us and not just the best *from* us. They root us on when we're going in the right direction yet they don't withhold correction when we're going down the wrong path. Don't stay in situations or relationships that slowly erode or take away from you striving to be better. Avoid pessimists, who only see the bad in everyone and everything, those who stay angry and argumentative.

- **Be Good To Your Body** - Reiterating and reemphasizing the link between our physical and mental health, get back to taking care of your body and it will help keep your mind fit as well. Feed your body real food not fake, disease-causing, addicting globs known as genetically modified organisms (GMO's). Their damages both short and long-term are becoming more and more visible, costly, and life-altering. These chemical concoctions threaten not only our physical health, showing up in the form or inflammation and toxicity but they've also proven to affect our brains as well. Coupled with regular or consistent physical activity and adequate rest and recovery, we can keep some level of sanity without as much wear and tear. This also means watch how you 'communicate' with yourself. Don't fill your head with negativity, doubt, and worry. Opt to use your liberty being thankful for where it comes from and speaking and showing it. Keep yourself at or near your best so you can continue to provide the best for those you love.

- **Reduce Stress** - Stress will be a part of our lives, one way or another. When it becomes too much to handle, the impact of stress on our mental health can be profound. The fact that stress will always be around should compel us to find a way to manage it or reduce its negative toll it can take on our minds. Developing quality coping skills will keep stress from dominating us and taking us away from living. Either by going for a walk or run, meditating, writing, or appreciating nature, you know, smelling the roses, you have to reduce stress. The fact that you have stress shouldn't make you feel picked on or like you have bad luck, your ability to stay balanced, focused, and thinking will be the difference.

- **Realistic Goal-Setting (Find Purpose)** - Do your actions on a daily basis match up with the goals you have for yourself? Do you still have goals and objectives for yourself? Do you have deadlines for your dreams? Accomplishing your goals will take planning and commitment yet we can be so busy and still not get anything done. If you are mindful of your purpose and take the time to write down your goals, daily, hourly, etc., goal setting and, thus checking progress, will be made easier. Get clear on purpose, plan it, and put it into practice. If your goals are realistic, you can be confident in your actions and be realistic in your expectations. On the flip side, if you don't have a purpose, you probably don't have a plan. If you are operating without a plan, you are more than likely unhappy and unmotivated with the inconsistencies you're experiencing. I know, personally, the frustration and mental anguish that comes from always trying to wing it or improvise and the comparative ease that is enjoyed when we are intentional and sure from start to finish.

- **Recognize When A Routine Is A Rut** - Very often a routine can be a security blanket or safety net as we grit our teeth, roll our eyes and give way to becoming zombies and slaves to clocks and schedules. Day in and day out we're shuffling through the same dread, and before you know it, we can become shiftless, thoughtless, and worn out wondering where the time is going. We can find ourselves in a rut, uncomfortable, uncertain, and mentally fatigued. Don't let the apparent comfort of a routine keep you from growing and accepting new challenges. Adopting new habits to break up the monotony might offer you the freedom you need to change your life completely.

- **Be An Optimist (Stay Grateful)** - When things are cloudy and darkening around us, it's critical to find the light at the end of the tunnel. To first recognize that things could be worse and then to be grateful that they are not, allows us to push through anything and maintain the right attitude in the face of challenges. Remember past successes, even small victories keep us hopeful and give us the opportunity to move from one obstacle or challenge to the next or develop self-efficacy. Even something we may think (at first) as simple as changing how you talk can be mentally strengthening. For example, I can recall a college professor at Abilene Christian giving the illustration of how we lose power with some of the languages we use like saying things like, "I have to this or that" or "I need to" or "I can't do this or that." Instead, say "I can" and "I get to" as this allows us not always to feel like pawns moved at the whim of everyone, but it empowers us. This keeps us from getting wiped out by life when it sends a screaming curveball. Being optimistic and positive makes it easier to get our bodies to follow the lead of our mind in pursuing the things that make for happiness, even in the midst of loss, sadness, and disappointment. It's a definite ingredient in more effective stress management and maintaining mental health. To see the best in people or viewing tough situations in the best light keeps us from making some bad situations worse. 'Losing heart' literally can kill you. Several studies, concentrating on the link between optimism and certain medical conditions, have shown optimism may protect the heart. Not only being less likely to be rehospitalized after a bypass is optimistic but similarly, highly pessimistic men were three times more likely to develop hypertension (high blood pressure) than their more positive thinking counterparts, even with other risk factors taken into account.

- **Avoid Alcohol** - Although those who choose to self-medicate with alcohol may stubbornly take the stance that drinking alcohol helps when they are feeling down, or it makes them feel like themselves again, do not neglect the fact that disorders related to alcohol use frequently disrupt the path of anyone, let alone someone with mental illness. It should not be forgotten or dismissed that according to pharmacology, alcohol is in the same category as other central nervous system depressants. Drinking alcohol can become addicting especially for certain groups with mental illness like men, folks of a lower socioeconomic status and veterans of the military. According to recent studies, almost a third of those with mental illness experience alcohol abuse while more than a third of all alcohol abusers are battling some mental illness. Alcohol abuse causes and worsens many mental disorders on top of the fact that alcoholism itself gets mistaken as a personality disorder at times. Alcohol not only causes depression and anxiety, but it mimics some of the recognizable traits of hopelessness and insomnia.

- **Get Help** - When you recognize things are getting or have gotten past the point where you can control them in a way that's not harming yourself or someone close to you, do not buy into the falsehood, the outright lie that asking for help is a weakness. People who get the care that they need can still recover and get back to leading productively fulfilling lives. Don't realize, too late, the strength that is shown when you seek and accept help. It just might save your relationship, your job, or even your life. Understand also, because it's for your betterment, it may seem that everything is working against it: help may be expensive, or may feel fearful or apprehensive, focus and find the help you need.

MENTAL WELLNESS

0 = Never or almost never (once a year or less)
1 = Seldom (2 to 12 times/year)
2 = Occasionally (2 - 4 times/month)
3 = Often (2 - 3 times/week)
4 = Regularly (4 - 6 times/week)
5 = Daily (every day)

1. I feel satisfied with who I am and where I am in my life.
2. I refuse to allow regrets and disappointments to ruin my day.
3. I feel a strong sense of connection with others and do not feel isolated
4. I tend to think rationally and optimistically
5. I do not hold onto grudges and can forgive others for not living up to my expectations.
6. I feel a great sense of control over my emotions, thoughts, and feelings.
7. I have a healthy sense of humor and can laugh at life's imperfections.
8. I feel more gratitude on how my life is now rather than focus on what's lacking.

Mental Wellness Score: _____

0-19 Poor/Low/Weak
20-29 Average
30-40 Strong/Stable/Excellent

FINANCIAL WELLNESS

"Keeping up with the Jones's" is a term I've heard probably since I was a kid yet I didn't fully grasp that concept or recognize the implications of that phrase until I was in high school. Who were these Jones's and why were they so important that everyone cared what they were doing? By no means am I some financial guru but how smart do we need to be to understand the ramifications of poor or no financial planning? The impact of that is evident when you look at the rise of personal debt, the credit crisis and seemingly there are just as many check cashing and payday loan spots as there are banks.

In fact, it's such big business that employers have implemented some form of financial wellness program to their offerings. Wellness programs already were proven to be a money and lifesaver for businesses looking to protect their main assets, their employees. This financial piece, though, which is now being offered or about to be at over 40% of companies, serves to alert and educate their employees about the financial risks they face and even offer risk management tools. The same strategies used to make the health and wellness program to be so successful have to be leveraged in this arena too.

There's an inherent link between being physically fit and

fiscally fit. Financial wellness is just as important as our physical fitness. Looking closer at it, when we struggle from a financial standpoint, the impact that has on our physical health is felt almost immediately. We tend to lead less healthy lives and incur the costs of those choices often in the form of extended medical visits and higher medical bills. Clearly, there's a lack of financial education because of how poor we are as health care consumers.

There's no substitute, from a financial standpoint, for having the peace of mind in knowing you control your finances. This has a significant impact on the amount of stress and anxiety, and indirectly how much sleep we get. When we are financially healthy, we are at least on that path where we benefit greatly at home and in the workplace. Along with improving our attitude and focus, we also benefit from improved performance on and off the clock when we have a strong financial wellness component in place. When we don't have to worry about the money part of our careers, we can focus on delivering quality service or performance.

In this economy, finances are always near the front of our minds, though. At home, it keeps the peace when you don't have to have the argument over money all of the time. At work, when you are financially well, you tend to be more satisfied and more productive as opposed to those who take their financial burden to work with them. Financial stress affects our attitude toward our work as we tend to have less focus and motivation when we feel we aren't financially being taken care of. We produce less and trend toward more carelessness, tardiness, and presenteeism than those who feel that their employers value them as more than just workers.

Budgeting And Managing Money

Wise money management is a series of choices and decisions that can't be discounted. A well-known quote states, 'If you fail to plan, then you plan to fail.' Financial wellness is definitely an area where that holds true. Once again, needs versus wants become a critical choice when it comes to budgeting. Money management and budgeting are two necessary keys to not only making good financial decisions but also achieving the financial goals we have set for ourselves. You do have financial goals, don't you?

Budgeting is valuable whether you have a lot of money or you're like many; you want to turn your little into a lot or even if the goal is just keeping what you have. This is your plan for the money you bring in and where it goes from there. No successful business will be as successful as it can be without having some working knowledge of both its income and its expenses. Why wouldn't the same apply to your personal finances as well? The road to financial freedom will be a long and rocky one if you know nothing of how much money you have coming in and how you get rid of it.

For most people, the immediate fear is that all of the extra fun and games will be eliminated. In reality, you probably will discover that certain things will no longer make the cut, but certainly, this is no reason not to sit down and look at real numbers. For example, without looking at your budget, how do you know you can't afford to eat healthier? More than likely, once compared to the financial risks associated with health costs, you can't afford not to.

Let the Jones's Be The Jones's

Although you wouldn't think so since many won't talk about it, far too many are living way beyond their means. As we just noted, to be financially healthy, you have to have an understanding of what you are spending in relation to how much you make. You must invest or spend less than you are if you're going to achieve the type of financial success you want. Between 1993 and 2008, according to the US Bureau of Economic Analysis, personal savings rates hit their lowest levels since the Great Depression in 2006, when it dipped into the negative territory. According to the same report, though, by May 2009, that rate had shot back up to 6.9%, is highest since 1993. The reason for that, according to the report, was because a recession hit right after we borrowed like crazy and that elevated consumer debt to its highest levels ever. A near global economic disaster plus that credit crisis was the only thing that finally slapped most Americans back to credit consciousness, but sadly it was too little, too late for most. By the end of 2008, bankruptcies filed nearly doubled according to the National Bankruptcy Research Center.

Clearly, even the Jones's were having a hard time keeping up with the Jones's suggesting that our best bet is to find and stay in our lane. Fortunately and yet, unfortunately, we are not the government and therefore can't take the liberty to operate beyond our means. We know people right now, or perhaps you're one who lives a life you can't afford, living on credit, and on the fast track toward not only a financial ruin but also an embarrassment. When we live beyond our means, we risk ruining not only or credit scores but also relationships and self-confidence. Besides all that, why fake the funk and risk being exposed as just a self-deceived fraud? Unless your name is Jones, mind your own financial business.

Here are a few questions to ask yourself to identify if you are, in fact, living beyond your means:

- Are you designer driven?
- Do you think a low paying job is "beneath you?"
- Is your credit score below 600?
- Are your bills still under control?
- Will your savings last at least a year?
- Do you VISA to vacation?
- Are you paying someone to do your menial jobs, unnecessarily?
- Are you over your credit limit and still counting?

Think about the answers to these questions and understand this is not automatic bankruptcy nor will you be thrown into Monopoly jail but rather view this as a free screening allowing you to self-diagnose before it inevitably gets worse.

Don't Let The Money Drive You

Ah, money: can't live with it, it's not living without it. As a society, we've always been somewhat money conscious, but nowadays we're more money focused. Don't misunderstand me; money is a necessity because we have to eat, pay bills, etc. but it should not be our main drive in life. Capitalism has given rise to greed and an increasing fear in a society where it's a common thing to be financially insecure and thus dependent on money for survival.

Money discussions and money concerns contribute to widespread depression, alcoholism, and panic and are becoming more of the norm than the exception. We live in a society that almost lulls folks who aren't even money-driven into being more money-centric because of its direct relation to our survival. There is less job security, higher rent/mortgage, tuition, not to mention the high food and healthcare costs, and we are left trying to figure out how much money will fix the situation (or at least make us feel better about it).

As part of the "younger generation" facing even less job security and the threat of no Social Security, we worry about never being able to pay off college debt. We fear of being the financial loser with all of this college debt, not even putting our degree to work. If we are "lucky" to land something in our field of study, will it even be decent paying and justify the debt?

It's been said, and we see for ourselves that the love of money is the root of all evil. When we are only about money, we will neglect everything else necessary to build self-respect and hang on to our integrity. This neglect eventually leads to the dissolution of trust and solidarity in business when it's revealed that you're dealing with someone willing to do anything for money. Having a money-centric focus directly tied to any belief or cause will weaken and eventually deaden even the most powerful idea.

So again, although money is necessary to survive, we shouldn't be willing to compromise who and what we are to accumulate it. Energy, passion, purpose and consistency are still valuable traits. They are what make us alive not the inevitable deterioration of making money more and more of our focus.

Avoid Credit Card Debt

Credit and thus credit card use are often viewed in a negative light, but it's for very good reason: if used loosely, it will lead to what can be a pretty formidable mountain of debt. Most of us will need to use credit at some point, but it's critical to remember that all credit is not created equally. Truly, any one of us carrying credit cards is at risks for collecting too much debt. Credit cards are high-risk, high interest "loans" that allow us to purchase whatever we want within your given credit limit without paying for it immediately. Seems simple enough right? It would do you well to remember that an overwhelming amount of debt can jump on you before you know it, so it's highly important to have some strategy in place to prevent this from taking place.

- **Limit the Number of Opportunities** -Doing simple math, we can see that the more cards you have, the more chances or, the more risks you'll run into since this allows you more opportunities to charge. Try to limit the number of open accounts to two maybe three max.
- **Be Clear About the Terms** - By reading through your card agreement, you'll help yourself in the long run by understanding the terms of the agreement. You'll have a clearer picture of how interest is accrued, when and what fees you may be charged, and when/if the interest is fixed or variable.
- **Pay In Full** - This may be your best bet to avoid collecting credit card debt. Pay the full balance off every month, and you won't have to worry about what the minimum payment is nor will you be suckered into paying crazy interest for years to come.

- **Pay On Time** - Late payments don't just damage your credit score, but you're also subjected to late fees, a changing interest rate, and it also goes onto your credit report.
- **Charge Only What You Can Afford** - Credit cards are not for financing an affordable lifestyle. You are overspending if you can't pay the entire (or most) of the balance within a month. Can't pay cash for it, don't charge it.
- **No Cash Advances** - Advances are a surefire way to get into credit card debt. Not only do they come with a ridiculously higher interest rate but you will also incur transaction fees and no grace period.

Think Long-Term Money

Think about your money in long terms. Set up a savings account. Start a Roth/IRA account or something similar to allow your money to work for you. To build wealth, it is essential that you find long-term investments. Learn how to diversify your portfolio.

In 1900, only 1% of Americans were into the stock market, and that number only increased to 4% by 1950. By the year 2000, well over 50% were in the stock market. Being financially smart and responsible in the short-term turns into long-term financial health. Smart people have made knowing what to invest in and what to avoid into a multi-billion dollar industry. Don't get too lost in those numbers, however, as recent history had shown us through the infamy of Ponzi schemes, that everyone can't be trusted. Your money is most important to you so I'd advise increasing your understanding of how to invest it wisely.

FINANCIAL WELLNESS

0 = Never or almost never (once a year or less)
1 = Seldom (2 to 12 times/year)
2 = Occasionally (2 - 4 times/month)
3 = Often (2 - 3 times/week)
4 = Regularly (4 - 6 times/week)
5 = Daily (every day)

1. I am comfortable leaving a balance on my credit card(s).
2. I think it is important to spend less than I earn.
3. I am confident that I can plan a financial budget.
4. I pay off the entire balance of my credit card(s) each month.
5. I have enough money saved to handle financial emergencies.
6. I track my spending to stay within my budget.
7. I feel stressed by the amount of money I owe (credit cards, student loans, etc.).
8. I stress about my finances.

Financial Wellness Score: _____

0-19 Poor/Weak/Low/Unstable
20-29 Average
30-40 Strong/Stable/Excellent

PHYSICAL WELLNESS

We have one "house" we get to live in for life, and that's our bodies. As we pursue physical wellness, we will seek to keep 'our houses in order' as we gain a better understanding and appreciation of what our bodies can do as we do more than just exist. At the same time, it is a high-performance machine and much like any other, without proper nourishment, support, and maintenance we can expedite our bodies toward breakdown and burnout. Physical wellness directly impacts our ability to fight off illness and disease and not just our ability to run a marathon or build a six pack. Physical wellness is how we measure our application of knowledge, skills, and behaviors against our commitment to self-management and achievement of our personal health and fitness goals. We count on our bodies for everything whether it be taking us to work, we use it in play, we fuel it, brings new life into the world, and probably not as much as we should, we let it rest.

Our society still places so much emphasis on physical appearance that it's lost sight of and the true value in leading a healthy lifestyle as opposed to reaching a reading on a scale. As a country, we spend more money on healthcare than any other country yet have more obesity and experience higher rates of preventable causes of death than any other country. Clearly, there's merit to the 12% national health literacy rate as the numbers of individuals battling weight issues, nutritional deficiencies, and the normalcy of lack of sleep continues to rise. Fad diets and celebrity-endorsed death traps continue to lure lovers of weight loss away from the education that puts the emphasis back on lifelong learning. Imbalances caused by cookie-cutter workouts and the growing nuisance of genetically modified organisms in our foods and drinks being consumed make for as much "chemical" confusion as muscle confusion.

Being physically well is an essential piece of the Total Wellness Pie as its influence can lead to psychological benefits like self-control/discipline, self-confidence, tenacity, and a sense of accomplishment. There's no one at any age that doesn't have an advantage by being physically and cardiovascularly fit. Kids and youth have been shown to make better grades and have better focus when they eat right and get sixty minutes of physical activity most days, if not every day. Young adults stay competitive and at their peak on and off the clock when they eat, work, and play with a purpose. Seniors are less likely to fall or develop certain diseases like Alzheimer's disease or dementia when they are active in their aging by eating nutritiously, maintaining strength, and consistently stimulating the heart. Clearly, the link between regular physical activity and our brain's health, our performance and how it relates to our success in preventing illness, injury, and exhaustion are undeniable.

Needless to say, the road to physical wellness at a time of insurance and health care change can be both chaotic and costly. The Center for Disease Control in 2011, estimated those costs at more than $8,600 a year while another study suggested obese individuals paid an estimated $1,400 more than individuals at a normal weight. It's more difficult than ever to create a healthy active lifestyle between increased public transportation, the gift and the curse known as technology. If that's not enough, since 1950, physically active jobs only make up 20% of the workforce while sedentary jobs increased by 83%. Your best bet is to develop a program that is fundamental enough that it doesn't overwhelm you yet multidimensional in that addresses more than just aesthetic and superficial purposes.

Move That Machine

I know that there will come a time that this body will begin to break down and will eventually come to an inevitable stop. Before that time comes, we have to take advantage of the "quiet" season, the preventative time before injury, stiffness, obesity, or age becomes a detriment. Your most complete and effective program not only addresses strength training, which should be done at least twice a week but also perform aerobic conditioning for the heart and pay consistent attention to flexibility. These three pieces make up a comprehensive fitness program with intensity, duration, and frequency being keys to its effectiveness.

Being physically active for 150 minutes a week or essentially thirty minutes a day on five of seven days at a moderate level helps us maintain healthy bones, muscles, and joints. A ten-minute walk has been shown to have the ability to alter our mood/attitude for up to two hours so I feel confident telling my clients that are customized program might affect you for the rest of your life. Physical activity helps cut our risks for some health issues like high blood pressure, heart disease, stroke, and even diabetes. Exercise is probably the cheapest but most effective preventative tool yet the most underutilized. Sometimes this is a product of ignorance where people don't know what to do while at other times folks opt for shortcuts in the form of magic pills, potions, creams and crippling contraptions that do more harm than good or nothing at all. There's no substitute for hard work nor can the results be discounted. Mental, emotional, as well as physical balance, are within reach when we can make exercising a priority. When we look good, we feel good. When we feel good, we want to do more. Injecting energy into your body will inject energy back into your life if you can move past being interested. Having a re-energized body and a sharp rejuvenated mind will take commitment.

Thinking about how much hard work, sweat, and sometimes tears it will take keeps many from proactively doing the best thing for themselves. They exaggerate the time it will take, assuming they need hours upon hours when in reality, the 150 minute a week requirement mentioned earlier, breaks down to not just thirty minutes a day but if you can't do thirty at a time, you can do three ten minute bouts. Can't lift heavy weights? Not a problem. Can't run or just don't want to? Not a problem. Not a CrossFit fan or don't like huge group fitness classes? That is still not a problem. Variety is not just the spice of life but adding some variety in your training will keep you focused, balanced and keeps you from getting bored or hitting the infamous plateau. One of the greatest things about the wide world of fitness is that there are many ways to get and stay fit and healthy. The following are the four types of exercises that should be included in your fitness program. Take note that they don't all have to be done every day but should be used to keep the routine from becoming 'routine.'

Balance Exercises

Having good balance is not just important as we age but rather significant as daily we're walking, taking stairs, jumping curbs, etc. Losses in balance occur when we trip, stand quickly or moving rapidly, so it's critical to try to preserve it. Balance exercises can be done as often as we want to but I would suggest at least three or more days a week regardless of age. Yoga, tai chi, and other balance training exercises will come in handy for aging individuals, obese persons, and stroke victims. Try balancing on one foot or using bosu or stability balls to challenge yourself.

Endurance (Aerobic) Exercise

Aerobic exercise or activity that increases your heart rate and breathing will keep your heart, lungs, and the rest of your circulatory system healthy and is an integral part of overall fitness. Biking, swimming, jogging, and boxing are all great options for endurance exercise. Once you build your endurance, doing many of your day-to-day tasks will go a lot quicker and smoother. As mentioned previously, the American Heart Association recommends at least two and a half hours or 150 minutes a week of moderate to vigorous activity. Some will be able to do more and others less so don't feel like you have to do as much as someone else. Have realistic expectations for yourself based on your health goals and capabilities so if that means doing only ten minutes at a time, just get it done. Start, then you can always add more time, increase distance and/or difficulty later.

Strength And Resistance Training

Throwing some weight around is good for more than just getting to grunt and slam heavy things into the ground. Resistance or strength training doesn't just help us look better and perform our daily tasks but also helps protect us from injury. Having more muscle also adds a little juice to your metabolic rate, so you burn more calories while you're resting. I'm not talking about you guys becoming Lee Haney or any of you ladies becoming G.I. Jane but at least twice a week train each muscle group. Don't corner yourself into doing heavy weights all of the time instead mix it up some and use free weights sometimes or machines. You can even do my body weight exercises like pushups or bodyweight squats which you can do anywhere. Choose the type and the time that works best for you. It's importance can't be understated. Your best-strengthening program increases bone strength and connective tissue as well as our muscles. Increased muscle mass, because it makes it easier to burn calories, also helps us maintain a healthy body weight and thus a better quality of life. I would recommend talking to a certified fitness pro to stay up-to-date on new techniques and programming as well as mastering mechanics to train more safely and effectively.

Flexibility Exercises

Stretching your muscles is probably one of the more underrated parts of many people's fitness program. Flexibility exercises may not turn you into a miler if you're a sprinter or turn you into The Hulk if you're Mr. Bean but being more flexible does keep our muscles lose and our bodies ready for other movements. Stretching is a must to alleviate stiffness and tightness and should not be neglected. As much as pain will allow or as far as is comfortable, keep the stretching smooth and slow. Remember to breathe deeply and normally for the duration of the ten to thirty-second stretch.

Food Is More Than Fuel

For years, I emphasized to individuals, families, groups and companies the necessity of proper fueling as it pertained to food intake. We've all heard that "we are what we eat" and perhaps never before has it been so difficult to avoid being cheap, fake, and empty. Between genetically modified organisms and myths like eating fat makes you fat or diet sodas are better/safer than regular ones, we, as consumers, are consistently creating chemical storms that erupt into the disease in our gut, our brains, and the development of certain cancers.

Malnutrition, by definition, describes both the individual who doesn't eat enough as well as the individual who over-eats. It's not always some emaciated kid with a swollen belly in a third world country that's malnourished. Obese and over-weight people right here in the U.S. are also a candid picture of malnourishment. Eating too much 'pseudo' food with little to no nutritious value causes inflammation and toxicity in our guts. We eat what we can afford, what's accessible, and what's convenient or we don't eat, unfortunately.

Proper nutrition is essential to growth in our youth and aids in maintenance as we mature. Over time, unconscious consumption of sugars, especially fake, as well as the saturation of processed food and the influence of alcohol begins to break through and show forth externally the decay it began internally. It shows up as type 2 diabetes in eight, nine, and ten-year-olds and as heart attacks and strokes in thirty-year-olds. According to Tiffani Hays, director of pediatric nutrition, education, and practice for Johns Hopkins Health System, about 17% of U.S. kids are obese. That's not a good sign for the future as that number is increasing and the sad fact that kids who experience difficulties in achieving the appropriate nutrients, in both quality and quantity, will also experience difficulty growing. That has to make them at higher risk for issues as they become teens and then adults.

Food and drink choices are now responsible for the genetic disaster, as studies show, suggesting that our genetic disposition and even our ability to fight disease can be influenced by daily choices. A groundbreaking experiment conducted by Duke University in 2000, showed an example of just how significant proper nutrition is in how genes are expressed. They used obese, diabetic mice that carried the agouti gene, so they were also at increased risk for cancer and had yellow hair. They were consistently fed foods high in folic acids and B-vitamins, also known as methyl-rich foods, prior and throughout their pregnancies. Their offspring, surprisingly, were *thin* and brown and the gene was also effectively repressed. This experiment describes a process called DNA methylation in which parents can increase or decrease their children's likelihood of suffering from certain diseases and conditions with what they eat. This methylation determines whether good or bad genes are expressed and plays a significant role in the modification of the bad genes' activities.

Our bodies are constantly sending us messages and responding to the things we do to it, yet we miss them due to ineffective listening or just not listening at all. We can get so caught up in trying to be a certain size or having certain superficial features that we can lose sight of the fact that being healthy should be the focus. When we eat the wrong things or pay no attention to the feedback from our body, we not only miss the message, but it can become detrimental and a bit overwhelming. Between the conflicting information regarding what's 'clean' or not, bottled water, and the ongoing debate over GMO labeling, it has never been easier to be unhealthy in our pursuit of becoming healthy. The line between too much information and too much misinformation has blurred and without a lot of effort, helplessness and confusion sets in. There are, seemingly, an endless supply of "quick fix" diets and celebrity-endorsed cleanses, detoxes, pills, and potions promising to help you flush your way to a slimmer, sleeker you. If you understand nothing else; so-called shortcuts and the focus on calories instead of chemicals has ruined America's waistline, left it with super digestive illnesses, caffeine jitters and brain tumors.

Leave the shortcuts for the road trips and traffic. You don't have to take shortcuts to start reaping the benefits of good eating and use nutrition as your best line of defense against disease and illness. Whether it's avoiding chronic degenerative illness or even putting age's effect on us in slow motion, eating with a purpose, according to a plan is the surest way to go. Everything from making sure you break that overnight fast to staying hydrated are essential principles to hold fast to. Here are a few more to keep in mind:

- **Limit Then Replace Sugar, Refined Carbs And Wheat** - All of us benefit greatly by avoiding adding sugars and consuming refined carbs. Nearly 70% of all Americans are overweight or obese, and sugar consumption is one major reason why. The average American consumes about three pounds of sugar a week or over 3,500 pounds over a lifetime. Comparably, in the 1820s, Americans only consumed about a twelve-ounce soda every five days on the average. Today that number is at about seventeen cans every five days. Despite those numbers, it's still surprising to learn that sugar is eight times more addicting than cocaine or heroine. According to Dr. Mark Hyman, sugar is the new nicotine. And worse, sugar causes diabetes and obesity. This addiction, like any other, leads us to make decisions that aren't fully under our control. Hyman believed that this inability to manage eating behaviors was due to hijacked biology and taste buds. I'm in agreement that these hyper-palatable, overly processed, over-sugared pseudo foods can begin to override what we might reasonably want to do, which is stop eating. Unfortunately, these foods turn the receptors off that are meant to alert us that we are full and we continue to eat and eat and eat.

- **Detox The Right Way** - Once those transmitters have stopped responding, you will help your body to reset those sensors with a good detox or cleanse. Detoxification is the natural process of eliminating processed foods and sugar and getting back to natural foods that our bodies are built for and better prepared to digest. Though our kidneys and livers are typically pretty good at their jobs, the detox is a good way to kick-start your "clean eating" journey. This provides your body with a nice solid foundation for your nutrition planning which would include real or whole foods. People tend to feel better after detoxification because they feel less fatigue. I always feel more energetic after it's done. The first time I did a seven-day detox, I didn't understand the full scope of what I was doing to my body. The second into the third day was the toughest for me as those were days I dealt with the head-throbbing reminder that my favorite drinks were no good for me. The headaches I experienced over those couple days was due to my body trying to readjust to not having my almost daily Dr. Pepper fix. Since all detoxes aren't created equally, it would be a good idea to get your doctor's permission before starting your detox. The detox I recommend is based on the consumption of fresh fruits, vegetables, nuts, seeds, beans, and lean sources of protein (after day 3). This, again, should be the cornerstone of your eating habits moving forward. It may not only add a boost to your sense of wellbeing and boost your immune system, but it may also improve your skin, hair, and gut health as you lose weight.

- **Cut Out Processed Foods** - Imagine eating fresh food that tastes good and is good for you without having to worry about where it came from or if it's even real food or not. Food, or what we've been led to believe is food, is not what it used to be. Genetically modified corn, soy, and wheat have turned the food industry and thus the health care industry, upside down. Up to 90%, roughly, of all the processed foods we see in typical grocery stores, have either corn or soy ingredients while white bread and other foods made with white flour are being consumed at an alarming rate. This highly processed versión of wheat is not only deficient in nutrition, but it's also insufficient to living up to the hype over whole wheat as a legitimately healthy food option. Many have fallen and do fall for label lies and diet deception, with the more recognized brand names in our country, predominantly, pushing product responsible for just as many deaths legally as cocaine, meth, heroin, and other illegal drugs.

Coronary heart disease, diabetes, cancer and stroke are only four of the top ten takers of life. These chronic diseases, albeit, preventable, can all be traced back directly to our consumption of Franken-foods. The quest for health by consuming processed foods is just as elusive as the belief that processed foods are even healthy. Calories were thought to be the biggest villain against reaching a 'normal' body weight. How disappointing to find so many dodging calories for the sake of reduced and "zero calorie" options only to still be unable to lose weight, be full, or even have confidence in what was healthy and was not. Labels on products claiming to be 'sugar-free' but still loaded with fake sugars like aspartame and high fructose corn syrup are examples of what we don't can most assuredly hurt us, if not kill us. Low-fat, low or no carb or fat-free on a label winds up being nothing but distractions and optical illusions. Our image of what we think healthy collides head-on with what we think food is, what it should taste like, as well as in what quantities to produce and consume have made for a game of Russian Roulette when it comes to eating. We appear to be losing. What positive outcome is to be expected when we intentionally are consuming food stuff that is designed not to rot, break down, or satisfy the needs of our bodies?

- **Don't Drink Your Calories** - Outside of drinking water, it will be difficult not to drink your calories. Personally, I would much rather chew my calories than drink them. All calories aren't built the same so even though there are 3,500 calories in one pound, the way you accumulate those 3,500 can be the difference between living a long, largely disease free life and just merely dreadfully existing. Our brains don't even register the things we eat the same as what we drink which is probably why it's so easy to consume too many calories when so many of them are being drunk, and we still eat the same as we normally would. Just as an example, a regular 8-ounce glass of orange juice typically has around 115 calories.

- **Fight Fat With Fat** - I know, I know it sounds out of left field, but believe it or not, fat consumption is not why but the majority of people for that directly or specifically. The problem is the consumption of the wrong fats, the consumption of saturated fats that our bodies aren't made to digest and have no purpose other than to be stored as fat. Consuming raw nuts, like walnuts, almonds, and pecans, and replacing some of the oil that you cook with coconut oil as your preferred fat will go a long way in reshaping both your body and protecting your brain.

Sleep

From the time I was a very young kid with my mom pleading with my brother and me to close our eyes for a much-needed nap (more so for her relief) until nowadays during my 'overly responsible' adult years when I crave that nap time, sleep has and will always have a very significant meaning for us all. It has changed the meaning and maybe even in quality over the years, but it has always been important. Sleep issues not only make our waking hours miserable but it also puts us at a greater or more heightened risk for death than heart disease, smoking, and even high blood pressure. Sleep problems like sleep apnea can make our quality of life a series of lagging and crashing, literally as studies show a lack of sleep is responsible for up to a fifteen fold increased the risk for a car wreck. Trying to operate on a day to day basis, period, on little to no sleep, can wreck other parts of our lives. Unfortunately, we've only peeled back a few layers in just how damaging it is and can be to our overall health without a plan.

At least forty million Americans every year struggle through the repercussions of chronic sleep disorders that wind up lingering forever while another approximate twenty million will go through sleep issues from time to time. Between sleep deprivation and other sleep disorders, the sixteen billion dollars in medical costs annually are nothing to wink at. That is just talking about the direct costs, so when you consider the indirect costs as related to our production and other factors, these numbers get even more eye opening. At its basic level, sleep time is recovery time for our bodies. We don't just sleep for the sake of sleeping, believe it or not. Our bodies heal over night and is a key cog in the wellness wheel as study after study show just how damaging lack of sleep is to our overall health. The link between sleep deprivation or sleep loss and obesity is becoming less blurry. A factor that we tend to not think of is sleep loss' contribution to excessive fat storage and obesity. Deeper than just the longer we stay up, the more we eat, we have to commit to this part of our health as much as we do our weight management portions.

We tend to discount something like snoring and regard it as simple, normal, or even as comical because we all know someone who snores and wakes themselves up snoring or we do it or have it done it to us. That snoring, though common place, very often goes untreated and undiagnosed until it becomes sleep apnea or worse, which is present in over 45% of the population. Sleep apnea is repeatedly stopping breathing in our sleep. That chronic snoring is also associated with an increase in some heart and brain-related diseases. Sleep apnea, in fact, is one of main risk factors for high blood pressure so if the snoring can be managed, so can the blood pressure which means a reduction in stroke risk. Nine percent of all adult women and an estimated 24% of men are believed to be battling some level of sleep apnea yet only a small percentage of them are even diagnosed or treated.

From a clinical or medical standpoint, the consequences or disadvantages of burning the midnight oil are costly, consuming, and constraining. Some of the more serious byproducts, other than high blood pressure and sleep apnea which was detailed earlier, associated with sleep disorders include but is not limited to:

- Heart attack
- Heart failure
- Stroke

- Psychiatric issues like depression and schizophrenia
- Fetal and childhood growth retardation
- Mental impairment
- Attention Deficit Disorder(ADD)
- Accidental injuries

As a general recommendation, it's suggested that we get seven or eight hours of sleep a night. Getting more specific, our mood, or inability to maintain a healthy bodyweight, and even our performance, whether in the bedroom or the board-room can be affected by sleep habits. More than eighty-five sleep disorders have been recognized by American Sleep Disorders Association with sleep apnea, insomnia, and rest-less leg syndrome being the most common, all with potentially devastating impact on us socially and professionally.

In the short-term, as far as what's been discovered thus far, some of the consequences of lack of sleep include:

- **Decreased Quality Of Life** - Certain activities that demand a lot of our focused attention probably won't be as fulfilling as they would be if you were rested. Try staying awake for the kid's recital or soccer game, watching a movie with the wife on date night, or even watching your favorite team play when you are sleep-starved. You may them watching you instead.
- **Hurt On The Job** - Do you work a job that demands razor-sharp focus and mental clarity like on a computer working spreadsheets or an assembly line working with small parts? What about operating machinery while unrested? Being overly sleepy on the job can leave you two to three times more likely to suffer a serious on the job injury.

- **Motor Vehicle Related** - Speaking of operating machinery while drowsy or sleepy, is there a more dangerous feat than *driving* a vehicle while *dozing*? Unfortunately, too many of us have been making "too good of time" to pull over and rest. I know I can recall a few of my brushes with becoming a part of the estimated 100,000 auto accidents a year. Driving while drowsy is also responsible for another 1,550 fatalities and 71,000 injuries a year according to the National Highway Traffic Safety Administration.

- **Impaired Memory And Cognition** - Part of the reason some of those accidents occur is that our ability to think straight or process the necessary things to maintain "normal" functioning are slowed or delayed. This impairment not only leads to long dreary days but we are dangerously less alert, so the likelihood of us remembering things, whether significant like stopping at a stop sign or slightly less significant like not locking your keys in your car are reduced. If you already suffer from lapses in memory, not getting enough sleep will not help the situation.

- **Strain Relationships** - Back in 2013, a study conducted at Ryerson University in Toronto showed that 30% to 40% of couples sleep in separate bedrooms. A large number of those split the sheets (and bedrooms, apparently) over snoring and other issues caused by one or both parties' sleep disorders. Nightmares, light sleeping, and conflicting bedtimes can be sources of disruption inside relationships. Edginess and moodiness, shortness of temper are already noted characteristics of people who don't get enough sleep. Think about your relationships, personally and even professionally. What's the quality of sleep you get on a regular basis and how is that affecting you or your relationship? Finding a solution to your sleeping ills can either help your relationship to feel like a dream or without it, it can continue to feel like you're sleepwalking through a nightmare.

The extent of how far reaching and profound the influence of sleep depravity on so many different aspects of our being has prompted researchers to equate that influence with that of the impact that alcohol has had on society. People engaged in at least a moderate bout with sleep apnea perform just as poorly as those driving drunk. Someone who's not well rested and drinks will become more impaired than the one who is well-rested. Many turn to coffee to get that caffeine fix to kickstart their day only to realize that caffeine nor any other stimulant can overcome severe sleep deficiencies.

Much of this suffering can be avoided, but obviously, information and awareness will play a significant role if we are to escape becoming another sleeping statistic. It may seem like no small thing, but if you aren't getting quality sleep on a consistent basis, you need to find out why or try to adopt new sleeping habits. Almost as quickly as I ask a prospective client about their eating and drinking habits, I like to find out their sleeping habits. As we've already discovered, not sleeping enough or getting below par and insufficient rest has a far-reaching impact on all of our lives, regardless of who we are or our age. Better management of our sleeping habits can make a major difference in our health, safety, and our wallets. What is your sleep routine?

Chances are if you have no idea what a sleep routine is, you struggle on a regular basis to get quality rest and people around you can tell. A sleep routine is just a fancy way of talking about how we communicate to our bodies at the end of the day that it is the end of the day and you're done with it. The process of getting a good night's sleep begins at least an hour before bedtime.

1. **Red Light The Blue Light** - Around an hour before you get ready for bed, turn off all blue light-emitting sources like your TVs, iPads, iPhones, computers, and tablets. Also, cover up any other flashing or blinking lights that may disturb you at night.

2. **Relax Your Mind** - Throughout the day we make some decisions, whether it concerns our job, our family, traffic, etc. so that by the time we go to bed, our minds are fried. An hour or two before bed, let those things go from your mind for the night. Don't just lay in the bed thinking and worrying. Instead, think calm or soothing thoughts while listening to some quiet music. Even as little as ten to fifteen minutes of relaxation may make a huge difference.

3. **Low-Brain Activity** - Try reading, soaking in a nice hot bath, meditation, or any other relaxation tool to make falling asleep easier.

4. **Shorten The Siesta** - Most of us do rest better at night, but I'd be lying if I said that I hadn't been bitten the mid-afternoon nap bug. My only problem was my "power" naps would last so long I'd wake up panicked, weakened and thought it was another day. I would suggest, then, keeping your naps under a half hour if you have to get a couple of early winks of sleep in.

5. **Don't Go To Bed Full or Hungry** - Going to bed after overeating or with an empty growling stomach will make a night in bed miserable and most uncomfortable. You don't forget to sleep, or at least going to bed, on an overloaded digestive system. Don't go to bed full of alcohol or caffeine either. Interruptions in your sleep have to be expected since the stimulating effects of caffeine and alcohol can take hours to wear off and robs you of deep and REM sleep. It may make you sleepy at first, but then it will increase the likelihood of you waking up more often overnight.

6. **Hit Snooze On The Sleeping Pills** - If you're one of the millions who has turned to sleeping pills in hopes that they'll afford you a quality night of sleep, I remind you that some of those sleeping meds are dangerous and habit-forming. Many have pretty alarming side effects that may last longer than the temporary fix provided by the pills, to begin with. They should only be taken as a short-term solution buying you time until you've adopted lifestyle changes that support your efforts to get a good night's rest.

7. **Sleep Til The Sun Comes Up** - It may not always be possible, but whenever you can, get up when the sun comes up. That natural light helps your body to reset it's clock daily. Open the blinds or curtains in the mornings and take in at least an hour of sunlight.

Master Management Of Stress

Stress? Has no one stress anymore, right? Between money issues, kid issues, and er uh underlying societal issues, I think most of us are pretty well acquainted with stress. What we don't all seem to understand is how to handle it and keep it from handling us. Stress can be good or bad much like our response to stress can be good or bad. In fact, 48% of all adults say stress has a negative impact on their lives, either professionally or personally. Without a plan on how to manage life's stressors, reacting to the physiological, emotional, and physical demands of stress can be overwhelming. For some, this poses the biggest challenge; the how. If we don't choose the right way to handle the things that give us the most stress and keep us awake the most at night, we only compound the problem. How many times has the boyfriend/girlfriend or husband or wife left angry, found alcohol, drove drunk and several lives changed permanently over something that started off as a disagreement over something they ultimately couldn't even remember, yes, that temporary.

Such is the "fight-or-flight" mode that goes off inside each of us every time our brain is alerted that we are "under attack." Despite what feels like a continual disappointment after discouragement after discord, at some point in there, we have to find some relief or release. The literal chemical release of hormones, meant for protection, wind up leading to more health, relationship, money, and generally, more life problems if we fail to find a successful stress shrinking system. This life does have a way of seemingly never letting up or giving us a chance to breathe, and our bodies' built-in release system doesn't get to shut off. We can't always wait until we are in the middle of a high-stress situation before we realize we either don't have a plan for handling stress or an ineffective or inefficient one.

Modern day necessities have made us all become multi-taskers and jugglers with the demands of home, work, relationships, and finances requiring our attention and care.

Identifying the stress and the stressors will go a long way in helping to keep its impact to a minimum (save a flare up here and there). When do you feel the most stress? What things cause you the most stress? Have they always caused you stress? How will you handle them in the future?

This is a lifelong thing, managing stress. As mentioned earlier, stress is not always bad or from a bad situation. My wedding day and graduation days were some of the most stressful moments in my life. All the hours, energy, effort, sweat was reduced to the longest, hardest heart-beating few moments that were over and a memory before I even knew it. The day your child, niece/nephew, or grandchild is born, while positive, can be stressful, to so say the least. Obviously, every day is not filled with high-level life events like that, well not for most of us. That doesn't mean that we don't have our daily doses of general stress, however, on the job or at home. This is why the popularity of stress management as part of successful corporate wellness programs is on the rise. Stress related health care and missed work costs employers approximately $300 billion annually. Some of the reasons behind that big number are more evident than others like but obviously just as damaging. I can vaguely remember a stat that stated stress was a contributing factor to anywhere from 75% to 90% of all trips to primary care physicians. One of my favorite stats to share with businesses relating to stress is that according to the U.S. Justice Department there are more than a million victims of workplace violence, which accounts for around 15% of all violent crimes. That aggression and violence is a typical staple of over-stressed individuals, so it's kind of an inevitable thing that it carries over from home to work and vice-versa. Unfortunately, those that aren't employed aren't excluded from being bitten by that violent and aggressive bug brought on by stress.

As a society, we seem to be more accustomed to the physical "acting out" associated with poor stress management but the passive aggressive nature of some won't allow them to respond physically. Don't underestimate the effect of prolonged passive psychological forms of aggression can have on an individual, a family, community, or an organization. Since I don't have the experience of living in the 50's and 60's, I only have what I've read and heard about what it was like to be black during those times when the threat and the physical act of violence was more pronounced than today. Nowadays, the attack is more covert and psychological, knowing that while you may not incur the same physical violence, you may be subject to technological threats and trauma via social media and sneaky things like that.

Moving on, stress has effects we see every day but don't associate with stress immediately like:

- **Stress Ages Us** - UC San Francisco research found that stress keeps new cells from growing as quickly leading to wrinkles, poor eyesight, weaker muscles and other signs of premature aging.
- **Weaker Immune System** -When our minds are stressed, our bodies can follow suit thus weakening our defense and immune system. Don't be surprised if you don't get sick when you're in need of some stress relief.
- **Natural Weight-Gainer** - The University of Miami conducted a study about stress on people that eat upwards of 40% more than they normally would. Funny, but in the hunter-gather days, the weather and terrain forced people to "load up" when food was available because they knew tough times would come.

PHYSICAL WELLNESS:

0 = Never or almost never (once a year or less)
1 = Seldom (2 to 12 times/year)
2 = Occasionally (2 - 4 times/month)
3 = Often (2 - 3 times/week)
4 = Regularly (4 - 6 times/week)
5 = Daily (every day)

1. I maintain a healthy diet. *(low fat, low sugar, fresh fruits, grains, and vegetables)*
2. My water intake is adequate. *(at least 1/2 oz/lb of body weight; 160 lbs. = 80 oz.)*
3. I am within 20 percent of my ideal body weight.
4. I feel physically attractive.
5. I fall asleep easily and sleep soundly.
6. I understand the causes of my chronic physical problems.
7. I am free of any drug or alcohol dependency. *(including nicotine, sugar, and caffeine)*
8. I engage in regular physical workouts lasting at least 20-30 minutes.
9. I have good endurance or aerobic capacity.
10. I practice breathing abdominally for at least a few minutes.
11. I set and maintain physically challenging goals.
12. I am physically strong.
13. I do some stretching and flexibility exercises.
14. I am free of chronic aches, pains, ailments, and diseases.
15. I have regular effortless bowel movements.
16. I go to bed tonight instead of tomorrow (by midnight).
17. I avoid or limit corn, soy, and wheat.

18. I prefer my own cooking over eating out.
19. I awaken in the morning feeling well rested.
20. I have just enough energy to meet my daily responsibilities.

Physical Wellness Score: _____

0-39 Poor/Bad/Highest Risk
40-79 Average
80-100 Excellent/Lowest Risk/Optimum

OCCUPATIONAL WELLNESS

If you could do anything in the world for a living and get paid for it, what would you be doing? Is that different than what you'd be doing if money were no issue? The occupational wellness piece has less to do with how much money we make than if it's in alignment with our values, morals, and desires. Confucius said, "Choose a job you love, and you'll never work a day in your life." Are you in a career that you enjoy, that's interesting and meaningful or is it just a paycheck? How does what you do contribute to those around you? Does it contribute or take away from the kind of person you want to be?

Occupational wellness focuses on not only our attitude toward what we do for a living but also about developing and utilizing our skills, gifts, and talents in a way that is beneficial and rewarding. This component highlights the importance of our choice of profession, our level of career ambition, and overall job satisfaction.

As we move forward here now and examine what occupational wellness looks like, let's be mindful of our current job situation and be able to recognize an occupationally unhealthy one as well.

Finding Motivation In Your Work

Are you able to find motivation in your job? Do you still find it interesting or was it ever? Personally, I've had jobs that no amount of money ever would have made me enjoy or appreciate. In fact, I've cringed and shuttered three times just since starting this section thinking about those jobs. The frustration and misery that comes from being unfulfilled is palpable. There's boredom, lethargy, and the monotony of doing the same thing day in and day out but never feeling accomplished. These jobs eventually take its toll on us. The coworkers are seemingly more annoying, the time goes slower, and soon you aren't interested in even being there. So what do you do to get it back when it's gone, and you can't just change jobs? Here are a few strategies:

- **Re-identify With What You Do** - Be clear on what you are there to do. If you can remember your "why" and what you're trying to accomplish, it should re-motivate you. Use a "goal sheet" to keep you focused throughout the day and review at the end of the day to see what and how much you got done.

- **The Significance Of What You Do** - How big a difference it makes when you are doing something important? It's a huge motivation to see the impact of what you do on those around you from your coworkers to those you serve. Do something that makes a difference. Whether you're a janitor, I'm sorry, a custodial engineer or a teacher, know that you make a difference.

- **Optimistic Office** - One thing that made my mad jobs mad was the amount of negativity that flowed through the workplace. When you already don't want to be there, you don't want to hear others verbalize their displeasures of their home lives or how much they can't stand this coworker or that boss. Focus on the positive and stay close to those who are like-minded and enjoy their jobs instead.

- **A Little Healthy Competition** - Coming from an athletic background, I can appreciate competition and see the built-in motivation that comes from outperforming my peers. In some industries, that's easier to do than in others, but a little healthy competition doesn't hurt. Who can fix a problem the fastest or seeing who's the most professional are ways of competing when you're not in an industry like sales where it's easier to measure the competition.

- **Strategize Skill Set** - Monotony is maddening and terribly unmotivating to sleep walk through the same thing day after day. If your job allows a little room for autonomy, you'll be able to identify and develop your personal skills. Stimulate your brain (and motivation) by structuring your schedule to be able to show the versatility of your skill set and stay engaged.

- **Long-Term Growth Focus** - It's tough to remain motivated at work when you feel like there's an invisible ceiling holding you down. Nearly all jobs have room to advance, so it's no wonder that when there's opportunity for advancement, either in position or pay, people get recharged. Even if not stated, attack your job like the bosses are looking to promote someone and you're the only one who knows it. You never know, they just might be.

Collaboration And Communication

Occupational wellness magnifies the importance of outstand-ing communication skills as well as seamless collaboration. Regardless of your job, effectively working with others is a necessity and the extent of your success depends on it. Effec-tive collaboration allows each to bring their best to table and from a company standpoint, what better situation to be in than to know you're part of a team willing to work together as a team for the betterment of all involved. This skill, accord-ing to top execs, is a "stand out" type of skill to have because even when you don't have the highest technical know-how, if you can listen and communicate with others, you can be as successful as you want to be.

When all members can share in the effort, both work and ideas, then the whole team, collectively, can run like a well-oiled machine. When all members feel like they are contributing, they can stay motivated and engaged every step of the way. Unfortunately, as sweet as this all sounds, it's not easy or always fun. Not everyone shares the vision all of the time. Some may want no parts of working on your team and perhaps there will be times and people you have no interest in working with. There are egos, some with stronger personalities than others, and obviously, some who won't have an appreciation of the process or your opinion on what they are bringing to the table.

Collaboration and communication come with their chal-lenges but, again, these are merely opportunities to grow and develop. When it works, it's a beautiful thing. When it doesn't, there's enough blame to go around. If you were baking a cake, there are certain ingredients you have to include in the mix to get that outcome: eggs, sugar, the mix, etc. The same is true for effective collaboration, which is, for as long as effective collaboration is the desired outcome.

Common Respect For Community Members

To effectively collaborate, all community may not like one another, but they must respect one another. In the workplace, it's easy to show respect toward those who we perceive to be smarter, who have more experience or make more money but what about those with whom that relationship is inverted. Can you maintain the same respect for all the members? You do expect it from them all, don't you?

- **Focus On The Results** - From the start, decide what success is going to look like. What can the whole team get behind to allow there to be constant progress? Identify the problem and the several risks or threats to that accomplishment so that when those problems arise, it won't stop the show.
- **Stay Authentic And Real** - This is almost an extension of the last key. If it's perceived that you aren't honest, being forthright, or as committed as the other members, respect and trust will wane. Keep it real at all times; you may earn more respect that way.
- **Cultivate A Culture Of Positivity** - Outside of working in a library or a funeral home; you want a fast-paced, dynamic environment with positive high energy. It's more fun that way and time flies by a lot faster when we aren't moving out of skepticism or uncertainty of the project or the people involved. If you don't observe these behaviors, perhaps your behaviors should reflect the vibe you're trying to create.

- **Stay Present And Engaged** - More than likely, you won't be talking all of the time. You may not talk very much at all. This is a problem for some who may find it difficult to stay engaged without their voice being heard all of the time. Listening and observing is what keeps up engaged, though, as it also reinforces the amount of trust and rapport with the whole group for the duration of the project.

So now that we've examined some of the essentials or characteristics of effective collaboration let's look at the other side of collaborating and communication coin: the communication piece. Effective communication is a key priority to ensure cohesive efficiency in our working relationships. To get the most from communication, setting the example and expectations from the beginning is essential to the long-term success of the unit.

As was just mentioned as an essential to successful and effective collaboration, active listening is a critical skill to master. This goes beyond just hearing the words but gaining an understanding and a connection with the communicator. Don't just keep your mouth closed til they finish talking. Give the effort in critical listening. This is key in the all-important "building of bridges," the main objective of communication. As the speaker, you aren't just talking; you are supplying the verbal nuts and bolts that connect you and your message to your listeners. Remember who's responsibility it is to make sure the right message comes across. It's not always about what we say but also how we say it since it comes down to what the hearers hear.

Communication itself, as a process is a vehicle for education. We use it to convey to folks what we see and/or what we want them to see. Depending on how well we do this, it may or may not compel them to do what we want them to do. Part of the job of the communicator is to know your audience and how you have to communicate with them whether this is speaking to a group or an individual.

We get into trouble when we forget that we are all different, so we learn differently, and we communicate differently. Be patient and slow down. We don't have to always rush through things despite life moving so rapidly around us. Specifically, we don't have to talk so fast that we rush through our message and can't even keep up with what we are saying. This drastically takes away from the clarity of our message as it gives the impression to the hearers that we are trying to sneak something in on them. Instead of coming across as untrustworthy because of rushed communication, here are three simple ways you can make your message a little more palatable:

- **Smile** - Whether you're communicating in person or over the phone, smile. In person, people tend to smile back, and on the phone, they can feel your smile which will relax them and help them to get out of any defensive mode or mindset they may be in.

- **The Eyes Have It** - Maintain eye contact whether you are the speaker or the hearer. From the speaker's standpoint, you come across as more trustworthy and honest. As a hearer, it shows (or strongly gives the impression) that you are tuned in and listening.

- **Nod** - While engaged in a conversation, try something as subtle as nodding your head, not like you're falling asleep but in agreement. Even on the phone, nod and use some reinforcements like saying, Yea/yes, ahh ok, and right."

Hopefully, this helps. Build the bridge effectively and watch success bloom right before your eyes.

Find Inspiration And Challenge In Your Work

Maybe it goes without saying, but hey I'm going to say it anyway; when you are inspired by what you do, you wake up excited to get to it. You are hungry for any challenge that comes because you realize the opportunity it provides. J.R. Martinez said, "I've learned in my life that's it's important to be able to step outside your comfort zone and be challenged with something you're not familiar or accustomed to. That challenge will allow you to see what you can do."

My worst jobs that I can recall were the worst because they didn't inspire me or challenge me…or so I thought. They inspired me alright, inspired me not ever to want to do those jobs again. My memory is at three right now, as far as the number of jobs that I can distinctly remember hating.

The first I remember loathing was my first job. I know you probably aren't supposed to love your first job, but I'm pretty sure you aren't supposed to hate it. I was about ten or eleven when my younger brother and I started working with cigar-chewing, racist ol' Joe Ellison on his farm in East Texas. If it wasn't bad enough that it was the heat of the summer and we were left all day to plant new seeds, pick vegetables and whatever other busy work his simple mind could come up with, he was the first white man we ever heard using the n-word. He wasn't just using it; he was tossing it around like we were on the set of *Django: Unchained*. On top of all that, the most he ever paid me was $25, unbelievably. Needless to say, those weren't the kind of challenges or opportunities I would encourage you to pursue. Forget motivation, inspiration, or anything positive because I honestly can't think of one good thing about either the man or his business.

Another job on my "work of shame" was a summer job I had taken the summer before I started college. It was at a "print art" company in McKinney, Texas, and I honestly wanted to quit the first day. My job consisted of working on a heated glue machine, again, in the middle of Texas summer heat with a "boss" who had no value in the company's main asset: the workers. The warehouse where myself and approximately ten Hispanic men and women labored in was without air conditioned but full of hot air and not just from the heat. The way he treated the other workers was shameful, and I was embarrassed for them. Although he never cussed me out or disrespected me as he did them, I couldn't be apart of anything like that especially since I knew that couldn't have been right. I did what I could to take up for them, but after two weeks, one day during a lunch break, I broke and didn't return.

The third and final walk down memory lane involved the first job I had right after college. After seeing several college classmates struggle to find work after completing their degrees, I was so worried I'd go the same route that right before my last year I explored career opportunities in Arizona. After that had fallen through, I went back and finished college. I went that whole year, so I could finish only to get that piece of paper.... and sell Kirby vacuums. I, too, had been bitten by the "Well what am I to do with this degree?" bug. I got fooled by the job opening headline that was looking for 'sports-minded' team players, and I had fallen for that. While I have no issue with anyone who may still be selling the Kirby dream, it wasn't for me. Although I had prior experience in sales, the fact that I had spent all of that time and money in college, psychologically wouldn't allow me to get comfortable in that field.

Needless to say, these experiences helped mold my views and opinions regarding occupational wellness and the importance of pursuing an occupation that challenged me in a way that would allow me to grow. I knew I had more to offer, and it would just be a matter of time before I'd be able to use my degree, my passion, and my talent.

Feeling Good About Your Work At The End Of The Day

You may be working somewhere right now where they don't appreciate you, you're limited to positives and benefits, and they neither pay you enough money or respect. You may not feel like you're doing something that's worthwhile or beneficial to anyone but the one's working you to death. Don't settle, know your worth. Take advantage of the opportunity to add to your skills, to increase your knowledge in an area of interest to you, one that you can put your whole heart behind.

After leaving the Kirby vacuum game, I continued to look for a way to put my college degree to use. About six months after graduating, I finally was given an opportunity. I completed a certification that encouraged me to start my career in the world of health and fitness. Soon after passing, I was employed by a private facility, connected with my first clients, and was finally getting to experience what it was like to enjoy what I was doing and getting paid for it. I now was inspired by the people who trusted in my skills and talents and no longer felt like I was a waste or was wasting time. I felt good at the end of the day and was excited about what challenges the next day would bring on the form of both challenges and new opportunities.

OCCUPATIONAL WELLNESS

0 = Never or almost never (once a year or less)
1 = Seldom (2 to 12 times/year)
2 = Occasionally (2 - 4 times/month)
3 = Often (2 - 3 times/week)
4 = Regularly (4 - 6 times/week)
5 = Daily (every day)

1. I find more satisfaction in my pay than my job.
2. I enjoy my career.
3. I contribute to those around me.
4. I dislike competition at work and don't view it as healthy.
5. I have and show respect for my coworkers.
6. My coworkers have and show me respect.
7. I feel like what I do has significance.
8. I am a team player.
9. I am inspired and challenged at work.
10. I feel good about my work at the end of the day.

Occupational Wellness Score: _____

0-25 Weak/Poor/Low
26-40 Average
41-50 Excellent/High

PUTTING IT ALL TOGETHER

Now that we've covered all of the dimensions of total wellness, naturally, you may have questions since it's a lot of information to take in all at once. Possibly some of this information is new to you, but even if it's not new, maybe it can serve as a good refresher or something that helps clarify areas of our well-being that you may not have been as familiar with. I have no problem admitting that years of working as a fitness and health professional, if someone asked what my definition or to give them an example of wellness, I don't know that I had an idea of what it was past the typical flu shots, working out or health screenings. I had no idea just how pervasive 'wellness' was nor how it mattered and just how significant a role it had already been playing in my life.

As you read through this, I hope you were able to identify with the pervasive nature of wellness and what it involves. Each aspect of our life involves some area of wellness. Many are so close and connected; you can't tell where one dimension ends, and the next one begins. Being from the Dallas-Fort Worth metroplex, it's one of the best ways to describe the versatility and completeness of wellness. You can be in Dallas one moment and Richardson, Addison or Plano the next.

The proximity of one town to the next one was so close you couldn't tell when you were in one or the other. To me, wellness is the same way. You can't address a physical wellness issue like weight loss without also addressing emotional or mental wellness in the process. Many of these dimensions or areas of wellbeing are similar and sometimes even connected to another, it just reminds you of how amazing we are as individuals and can be as a collective.

Whether you are young, old, man, or woman, you've experienced something that has knocked you to your knees or forced you to scramble to find your right mind and footing again. There are people hurting around the globe, but just as certain, there are people doing the hurting globally as well. Whenever we think we're doing bad, someone somewhere is doing worse. Suffering and loss are real and come with real consequences. At times, the healing takes a longer time because we don't allow time for healing or we trust too much in our own abilities to save or dislodge ourselves from what binds, confines and restricts us.

By no means, are the words in this book the end-all cure-all nor was it written to gloat, high-side, or lead anyone to believe that I have all the answers. I'm no different than you in that I've been hurt, I have hurt others. I have failed. I have lost. I have stumbled. I have lied and been lied to. I misunderstand and have been misunderstood. We have neighbors, friends, family, and others we walk and talk with, maybe even on a daily basis, who are going through things we can't even comprehend. It's so easy to just go around treating folks out of our own reality, completely oblivious to the fact, that we, in our own lives or mind, are not the center of the universe.

Scripture in the book of Romans in the New Testament

of the Bible says, 'for none of us lives to himself and no man dies to himself... whether you live, therefore, or die, we are the Lord's. We aren't all here to please our self, but our Maker and even our neighbor before ourselves. Money is good and necessary, but that can't be the focus always. Are we empowering one another or are we, in our own several ways, bullies to those we perceive as weaker or 'less important, less significant, and less of people or person than we are?

We are all the stars of our own reality show but we're the only one with the script. Sometimes people don't say or do the things that you think that they should. How could it not happen when they don't have the script to your show, and undoubtedly, they're trying to write and still star in their own show. The bottom line is we never know what the next person is going through or has gone through and more significantly, we have no idea what they will go through. We experience loss, failure, disappointment, and delusion from time to time in this life. Recovery is key. Full recovery takes a lifetime and that's if we are lucky. Many families, including my own, are all too familiar with the stains left by suicide. We scramble, searching for the answers from someone who will never reply. We are all bouncing back or have bounced back, but most assuredly there will be times, in the not-so-distant future, that we will all have to bounce back from something or another.

We see the hatred, prejudice, hypocrisy, and the hiding of hands while becoming more and more desensitized or turning a blind eye to violence. They say 'he or she might have deserved it' so they justify sitting back in silence as another woman is dragged by her hair, publicly, punched, choked or kicked by some overgrown coward with no coping skills.

We pick and choose our battles but it can't only be when we, personally, have something at stake. Too often, sadly, people, while whole communities are being disenfranchised, care more or give more consideration to what happens to animals than that of human beings. Social media is full of it. In 2016, the deaths of an alligator, numerous pets left in vehicles, and a gorilla made more news and created more of an uproar than the public shooting deaths of unarmed men and women and the severe neglect and mistreatment of veterans. Countless comments, live videos, and memes flooded timelines documenting the disgust and outrage of the 'inhumanity' shown to the animals from folks whose silence spoke volumes when inhumanity was on full display in actions against humans.

We are all conditioned to love, like, trust, etcetera people who look like us or act like us but the greatest love one that unconditional, enduring, and hopeful. When calamity comes or loss, it's a shock to the system sometimes. At times, it takes a while to shake it off and regain the focus needed to overcome when we want it immediately. We are all different, unique individuals who learn differently, have differing values, opinions, outlooks and ambitions. We have our ideals of success, comfort, and living and far too often, we can't ignore the fact that we can't force those ideals upon anyone, regardless of how well they fit into our lives.

From what are you bouncing back? What have you bounced back from in your time here on earth? We are fighters and overcomers, consistently faced with situations that challenge our foundations and make it difficult to be comfortable in this life. Change is constant yet with a plan or with the appropriate buffers; we can be better at handling changes that otherwise wipe us out.

The statements on the next couple pages will allow you

have a clearer picture of what total wellness looks like and how well you are taking care of your whole being. There are statements pertaining to each dimension of wellness, so statements will range from how grateful you are for your blessings and sense of belonging to your quality of sleep and your attitude towards anger or fear. Each statement is worth up to 5(five) points apiece and a 0(zero) is possible. Add up your points at the end to determine your Total Wellness score.

MEASURING MY TOTAL WELLNESS

0 = Never or almost never (once a year or less)
1 = Seldom (2 to 12 times/year)
2 = Occasionally (2 - 4 times/month)
3 = Often (2 - 3 times/week)
4 = Regularly (4 - 6 times/week)
5 = Daily (every day)

SPIRITUAL AND SOCIAL WELLNESS [SPIRIT]

1. I actively commit time to my spiritual life.
2. I take time for prayer, meditation, or reflection.
3. I listen to my intuition.
4. Creative activities are a part of my work or leisure time.
5. I take risks or exceed previous limits.
6. I have faith in God, spirit guides, or angels.
7. I am free from anger toward God.
8. I am grateful for the blessings in my life.
9. I take walks, garden, or have contact with nature.
10. I am able to let go of my attachment to specific outcomes and embrace uncertainty.
11. I observe a day of rest completely away from work, dedicated to nurturing myself and my family.

12. I can let go of my self-interest in deciding the best course of action for a given situation.
13. I feel a sense of purpose.
14. I make time to connect with young children and/or older relatives, either my own or someone else's.
15. Playfulness and humor are important to me in my daily life.
16. I have the ability to forgive myself and others.
17. I demonstrate willingness to commit to a marriage or compatible long-term relationship.
18. I confide in or speak openly with one or more close friends.
19. I do or did feel close to my parents.
20. If I have experienced the loss of a loved one, have I fully grieved that loss?
21. My experience of pain enables me to grow spiritually.
22. I go out of my way or give time to help others.
23. I feel a sense of belonging to a group or community.
24. I experience unconditional love.

Total 'Spirit' Score: _____

EMOTIONAL AND MENTAL WELLNESS [MIND]

1. I have specific goals in my personal and professional life.
2. I have the ability to concentrate for extended periods of time.
3. I use visualization or mental imagery to help me attain my goals or enhance my performance.
4. I believe it is possible to change.

5. I can meet my financial needs and desires.
6. My outlook is basically optimistic.
7. I give myself more supportive messages than critical messages.
8. My job or career utilizes all of my greatest talents.
9. My job or career is enjoyable and fulfilling.
10. I am willing to take risks or make mistakes in order to succeed.
11. I am able to adjust my beliefs and attitudes as a result of learning from painful experiences.
12. I have a sense of humor.
13. I maintain peace of mind and tranquility.
14. I am free from a strong need for control or the need to be right.
15. I am able to fully experience (feel) my painful feelings such as fear, anger, sadness, and hopelessness.
16. I am aware of and able to safely express fear.
17. I am aware of and able to safely express anger.
18. I am aware of and able to safely express sadness or cry.
19. I am fully accepting of all my feelings.
20. I engage in meditation, contemplation, or psychotherapy to better understand my feelings.
21. My sleep is free from disturbing dreams.
22. I explore the symbolism and emotional content of my dreams.
23. I do take the time to wind down and relax, and/or make time for activities that are recreational.
24. I experience feelings of exhilaration.

Total 'Mind' Score: _____

PHYSICAL WELLNESS [BODY]

1. I maintain a healthy diet. (*low fat, low sugar, fresh fruits, grains, and vegetables*)
2. My water intake is adequate. (*at least 1/2 oz/lb of body-weight; 160 lbs. = 80 oz.*)
3. I am within 20% of my ideal body weight.
4. I feel physically attractive.
5. I fall asleep easily and sleep soundly.
6. I awaken in the morning feeling well rested.
7. I have just enough energy to meet my daily responsibilities.
8. My five senses are acute and sharp.
9. I take the time to experience sensual pleasure.
10. I regularly schedule a massage or deep-tissue body work.
11. My sexual relationship feels gratifying.
12. I do engage in regular physical workouts lasting at least twenty minutes
13. I have good endurance or aerobic capacity.
14. I breathe abdominally for at least a few minutes.
15. I maintain physically challenging goals.
16. I am physically strong.
17. I do some stretching exercises.
18. I am free of chronic aches, pains, ailments, and diseases.
19. I have regular effortless bowel movements.
20. I understand the causes of my chronic physical problems.
21. I am free of any drug or alcohol dependency. (*including nicotine, sugar, and caffeine*)
22. I live in a healthy environment with respect to clean air, water, and indoor pollution.
23. I feel empowered or energized by nature.

24. I feel a strong connection with and have an appreciation for my body, my home, and my environment.

Total 'Body' Score: _____

Total Wellness Score: _____

(0-120) Wow, I really have some work to do but I know I can do this! My style of living is not toward my betterment.

(121-240) Just a few more tweaks but I'm headed in the right direction. I'm confident in the changes I'm making.

(241-360) I'm fully aware of the importance of my whole health. My behaviors and attitude support me as I continue living my longest, healthiest and most successful life.

www.ingramcontent.com/pod-product-compliance
Lightning Source LLC
Chambersburg PA
CBHW071131250626
47159CB00006B/2203